UNDER THE GAZE OF ANGELS

UNDER
THE
GAZE OF ANGELS

stories
SAID HABIB

Interlink Books

An imprint of Interlink Publishing Group, Inc.
Northampton, Massachusetts

First published in 2021 by

Interlink Books
An imprint of Interlink Publishing Group, Inc.
46 Crosby Street, Northampton, MA 01060
www.interlinkbooks.com

Library of Congress Cataloging-in-Publication data available
ISBN-13: 978-1-62371-899-2

Printed and bound in the United States of America

For my daughter Isabel and my son Jamil

CONTENTS

Zuha and the Book Vendor

Zuha did what she had vowed to do on the day her husband died. After midnight, she went to her hope chest and, from under a stack of linen sheets, took out the sleeveless blue dress that she had sewn in secret. The dress was fashioned after a photograph of a British model that she had seen in her husband's wallet, protected by a clear plastic cover sewn into the leather. Zuha put on the dress. She untied her long dark hair that she wore in a single braid so that it fell delicately on her shoulders. With a pounding heart, she walked under the cover of the night sky to the cemetery and danced around her husband's grave. She swayed her body provocatively, in defiance of a man who had controlled her every move. Zuha was aware that other women vowed to dance on their husbands' graves as an expression of their displeasure with them. But as far as she knew, she was the first to actually do so.

Upon returning home, Zuha unlocked the large door which led to the courtyard. She was met with the sweet-scented air that had been trapped behind the high walls of her garden. The walls were built long ago by her dead husband's departed father to contain his wife and to prevent her sight from wandering beyond her domestic chores and his needs. Unaccustomed to being in the courtyard so late at night and bewitched by the crescent moon in the sky, Zuha sat on the little bench close to the jasmine shrub and looked up. The jasmine, perhaps driven by desires of its own, climbed all the way to the top of the wall, and then draped its intricate branches and beautiful flowers onto the exterior side for passersby to admire.

Unable to have children, Zuha had poured her energy into the garden, in hope that its beauty would be a small compensation for her and her husband to enjoy. But he had never noticed the garden or his wife's gentle nature. He was only preoccupied with the desire to have a boy. Other men had started to question his virility behind his back, for most women in Baradi were with a child after the first year of marriage. Remembering her husband's nightly arguments and his cruelty, she wept happy tears. Realizing that it was never going to happen again, she removed her sweat-drenched dress from her quivering body, then moved closer to the jasmine shrub. Feeling the sensual pleasure of its flowers against her skin, she plucked the fragrant white blossoms and caressed them against her body. Tired, she walked into her house, still covered with flower petals, and soon fell asleep.

Still asleep, she heard the sound of the brass bell that was mounted above the courtyard door. She brushed off the jasmine petals before putting on her housecoat, and went to answer the door. Her neighbor had come to offer condolences and to help Zuha receive mourners. Surprised and annoyed by the floral scent in the room, the woman looked at Zuha reprovingly before opening the window, which let in an even sweeter scent into the room. Irritated by the perfumed air, she slammed the window shut.

Zuha received her neighbors' condolences with a mixture of gratitude and anger. Men, with their hands raised to their hearts, spoke of the virtues that her husband had possessed and of his devotion to God. Ashamed of their doubts about his masculinity, they fabricated stories about his heroic deeds. Not for Zuha's sake, but as an apology to the dead man and for their doubts about his virility for not having a child. They held the superstitious belief that the deceased have knowing power and can exact revenge on the living.

After everyone left, Zuha locked the large courtyard door. She began to rearrange the furniture. She removed the large obligatory photo of her dead husband that had dominated the central wall in her living room. She stripped the bed on which he died from a heart attack and began to wash the sheets that contained his smell. She felt happy and free, a feeling that she had not experienced since childhood.

It didn't take long for her to accept her new independence. The self-reliance inherent to her character had only been subdued by marriage. Although it was only the beginning of her forty-day mourning period and too early for her to resume her work as a seamstress, she moved her sewing machine to a new spot near the window and began to sew a black mourning dress for herself. It was an offering to custom, and nothing more.

Zuha felt happy behind the walls. She had no desire to leave. She loved working in her garden, sheltered from probing eyes. Her daily food, delivered by women in the neighborhood, allowed her to remain inside. Soon she found that she had more food than she could eat. Sometimes women came in a group and marveled at how happy she seemed. Perhaps they even envied her position. She had a house and a means of livelihood. They looked at her beauty with admiration, though her black dress was over-sized and meant to hide the contour of her body. The women who in 1927 came to Baradi from Zatoni, her village through marriage, knew what was under the dress. They still remembered the day before her wedding, when they had to prepare her for the groom. They remembered the waxing party at her mother's house. They remembered how beautiful and smooth her skin was. Although the waxing was unnecessary, they still went through with the ritual. The henna was reluctantly applied to her perfect hands that had no need for decoration. Above all, they admired her green eyes, for such eyes were extremely rare. Not knowing the history of the pillaging crusaders in their country, the women mistakenly assumed that her green eyes were a gift from a loving God.

After the death of her husband, Zuha seemed at first like those birds in the market that have known no other life than captivity. The door to their cage is left wide open, yet they choose to remain inside. She was aware of her self-imposed restrictions, and also of the societal expectations that demanded respect for the dead. Inwardly, however, she questioned how even an immoral person is somehow redeemed in death, as seemed to be the case with her husband.

Zuha thought of her mother, whom she hadn't seen in thirteen years. Zuha's husband had refused to let her visit Zatoni, where her mother lived, even though it was only an hour away by bus. Zuha decided that the first thing she was going to do after the forty days of mourning had passed was to finally make a visit. She recalled how she had depended on travelers from her village to bring news of her mother, since her pleas for permission to travel there had been ignored, even mocked. Her husband often taunted her, saying that her old mother's breasts were too dry now for her to suckle.

Without her husband's overseeing, Zuha had leisure to revel in the activity she loved most: tending to her garden. The flowerbeds blossomed profusely, rewarding her efforts, but the shallow pool that had once been stocked with goldfish was empty. She wished to go to the market and get goldfish. But she couldn't; tradition was still acting as her dead husband's proxy, if only for the next forty days.

On the second week of his passing, she allowed herself a visit to the food market: a necessity deemed acceptable by the people in her village. Walking back from the market, she noticed things that she hadn't before. It felt as if it was her first walk through a street that had been her regular route for many years. In the past, her outings would be hurried with her eyes cast downward, but now she could look at her surroundings. Walking by the book vendor's carpet, she quickly examined the vendor. He wore wire-rimmed spectacles and a tie that was pinned to his shirt. By virtue of his trade, he looked different from the other disheveled men of the market. His books were neatly stacked on an old Persian carpet spread on the sidewalk. She couldn't stop to read the titles, but knew that she would return as soon as she was free of her restrictions.

Zuha welcomed the sight of her house when it appeared in the distance. She could see its graceful arches peeking over the courtyard walls. Sitting in her garden, she felt an over-whelming desire to see what was behind the door that led to the rooms where her in-law's used to live. She decided to open it. The walls in the living room were a light shade of blue, and the furniture in it was carefully put together. Except for the colorful Persian rugs, the room had little decorative embellishment. The same elegant simplicity was carried throughout the space. Zuha had never known her husband's family. She wondered how her husband turned out to be so boorish, growing up in such a refined environment.

After closing the door, Zuha went back to her own living quarters and sat at her sewing machine. Wanting to see if it was still in good working order, she placed her feet on the pedal. She listened as it began to hum. Imagining that she was moving forward through time, she pedaled faster and faster, and didn't stop until her feet began to ache. Feeling silly, she moved to her cutting table and began to cut fabric for a new dress. She took more care this time. She wanted this dress to reflect the skills of which she was immensely proud. Upon completion, she pinned the hem of her new dress a fraction shorter than she would normally. Looking in the mirror, she decided to move it up just a little more. Her dress finished, she decided to wear it simply for her own pleasure.

She was looking at herself in the mirror when the bell swung above her front door. A middle-aged man stood on her doorstep. After greeting her, the man said that he was from Zatoni, her home village. He explained that her mother had heard about her husband's passing and was concerned for her well-being. Assuring him that she was fine, she said that she would soon be visiting her mother, and thanked him for bringing the message.

Zuha welcomed the end of each day and waited for the next to bring her closer to the end of her mourning. In anticipation, she decided to separate her work space from her residence. She made plans to move to the section of the house where her in-laws had once lived. It was nicer, and devoid of memories. Her living room would transform into a workspace, and her old bedroom would become a guest room. The kitchen adjacent to the sewing room would be for making coffee for her clients. No one would see her living quarters, and she would have absolute privacy.

In preparation for the move, she went to bed early and was up the next day at six in the morning. The sun beamed on her garden, and she could feel its warmth filling her with energy and joy. Cleaning the new living space made her forget the calendar. She imagined all sorts of possibilities. She began to design a sign small enough to fit on the exterior panel of her courtyard door. She took a pencil and scribbled on a piece of cardboard, trying out different designs. Feeling emboldened, she wrote, "Zuha's Dressmaking Shop." She liked how it looked. She felt delirious with excitement. The possibilities were immense. That night, she went to bed with her mind brimming with ideas. The morning sun cleared her head and brought her back to the reality of her culture, and she made an effort to erase the sign from her memory. She even felt slightly embarrassed at having dared to imagine her name on a sign that every man in her village would see.

With few days of mourning left, Zuha began the preparation for her visit to Zatoni. When the day arrived, she packed a suitcase and was about to leave her house when the bell above her courtyard door swung rapidly. Lifting the latch, her friend, Nabila, rushed in and took shelter behind her back, pleading for Zuha to protect her from her raging husband who was trailing behind. Knowing that there was no man in the house, he burst into the courtyard and saw his wife cowering behind Zuha. Nabila's strategy worked. Her husband, Yousef, came to a full stop. Disarmed by Zuha's beauty, he stood there fumbling for something to say. Then he glared at his wife angrily and walked out. Nabila asked if she could stay for a while, at least until her husband's anger had subsided. Zuha sat her by the fountain and listened as Nabila expressed her sorrow that her daughters had to witness Yousef's verbal abuse, and her own inability to stop his rants.

As the bus moved away from Baradi, Zuha, who had been rooted in her house for many years, felt nervous. Her uneasiness about leaving her house grew worse on the bumpy road, which made her queasy all the way home. When she arrived in Zatoni, she walked with her head down, remembering a path that she knew by heart.

Her mother, Amina, like so many older women of her generation, lived without any expectations. For her, things happened when God willed them to happen. She thanked God for returning her daughter to her. Much had changed since their separation. They spent the first few days reminiscing about their distant past. Sitting with her mother, Zuha tried to sort out her emotions. She'd only been with her for a short time, but it seemed that her mother had run out of things to say. Zuha felt confused when she realized that she didn't have much to say to her either. And yet, her mother seemed satisfied to just be with her. To break the silence, Zuha invited her mother to Baradi, with a promise of pleasant times in her garden. But her mother was reluctant, accustomed to her quiet life, and said that she was happy at home. Failing to entice her mother with pleasure, she tempted her with duty. "I could really use your company during this difficult period in my life," Zuha said. It worked, and the old woman accepted the invitation.

The news of Zuha's visit to Zatoni spread quickly. Old friends came to see her. Following a long-established code of behavior, they restrained themselves from laughter or light conversation, offering her condolences for the loss of her husband. Salim, a childhood friend who lived next to her mother's house, also came to visit, bringing his wife and three children. Zuha remembered playing with him when they were young, climbing trees and picking wild flowers. She had secretly believed that he was the boy she was going to marry. Happy to be with her friends, Zuha vowed never to be separated from them again.

Sitting on the bus, Zuha's mother appeared to be at ease, even happy to be traveling after so many years at home. When they arrived in Baradi, Zuha left her sitting in the courtyard and went in to prepare a meal. Shortly after dinner, her mother said that she was ready for bed, though Zuha was longing for conversation. All Amina could offer her daughter was silence. The next morning, Zuha woke up to find that her mother was already in the kitchen making coffee and whispering her daily prayer. Afraid that she would be asked to join in, she went back to her room, put on her work dress, and walked out to her garden. She no longer said her prayers. Communication with God had stopped after her marriage to a man who demanded all of her devotion.

Zuha was happy to have her mother with her. She felt strong when they went to the market. Having her by her side gave her the courage to stop near the book vendor's carpet. She hesitated at first, and it was not until she heard his greetings that she stepped onto the carpet. Feeling like someone who had ventured into forbidden domain, Zuha's heart raced. Her husband had forbidden reading. However, she quickly bought the first book within reach.

Zuha's quiet house came to life when friends and neighbors came to greet her mother. Discovering that her daughter was happy as a seamstress, and seeing how much affection she received from her friends, made Amina happy. Later in the week she was able to bid her daughter farewell knowing that the visit made them both stronger.

While cleaning the dresser drawers one morning, Zuha came across her husband's wallet. Her heart beat faster when she remembered how she had once found his wallet left open on the dresser, and how she quickly copied the model's dress on a piece of paper while her husband showered. Except for the few coins in the little pouch, the wallet was empty. It was as though he had carried it only for the photo's sake. Free of fear, she stood there and examined the model more carefully. She noticed the flowing hair, and the bright red lips smiling as though without a single care. She wondered just how often he had looked at the picture. Had he desired this woman? He expected her to live a life of piety, and yet he had walked around carrying a picture of a free woman in his pocket. It was so absurd that it made her angry. She placed the wallet back in the drawer, went to her sewing machine, and resumed her work, but she was ill at ease. She recalled how her mother had lived her entire life without any aspirations and accepted her submissive life without protest. Zuha did not want the same fate. In an act of defiance, she decided to display her secret blue dress. She hung it on the wall in her sewing room.

Seeing the dress, some of her friends wanted one like it. They were willing to pay anything she asked, as long as she would keep the secret dresses in her house and away from their husbands. They selected bright colors and a variety of forbidden styles, and waited in anticipation while Zuha sewed. Energized by excitement she had never felt before, Zuha worked into the late hours day after day. Finally, when the dresses were ready, she invited the women all together, and locked the main door that led to her courtyard. Wearing their new dresses, the women sat in the garden, drinking mint tea, looking demure but feeling rebellious. It seemed as if this gathering was a rehearsal for things to come. Zuha knew that the secret meeting in her garden was just a whimsical reprieve from everyday realities, but she hoped that future gatherings would serve as an exercise in self-expression.

Noticing a book on the small table where Zuha often sat to read, one of her friends inquired in a sly tone if the book vendor was happy to see her on his carpet.

"He is happy to sell his books, and as far as I can tell, he is not happier to see me than he would be to see any other client," responded Zuha.

"The man must surely be blind," said her friend. "If I were a man, I would be lighting a candle by your image on every day of the week." Zuha laughed and put the thought aside.

Once the dresses were completed, Zuha spent her evenings reading, sometimes past midnight, unaware of the time, absorbed in stories from faraway places. She was eager to read more but feared that stopping at the carpet too often would be seen as inappropriate. She walked to his carpet, resolved to buy two books at once.

Aware of her haste, he selected a book by the Lebanese poet Kahlil Gibran, and said that she might like it. Blushing at what seemed like intimacy, Zuha paid for it without looking and left in a hurry.

Walking home, she felt as though the book in her purse was now acting as a liaison with a man she hardly knew yet felt deeply attracted to. She entered her courtyard, locked the door behind her, then sat near her jasmine to read. When it was dark she went inside, lit the oil lamp, and continued to read in bed until the oil ran out. Then she fell asleep.

The book returned to her mind in the morning, and even then she could feel its transformative effect on her. She was still daydreaming when the bell swung over her door. She rushed to the door and found Nabila standing alone.

"I'm glad that he's not after you," Zuha said, relieved. "I'm not in the mood to humor him again." Nabila said that she only wanted to put her secret dress on for a while.

Zuha understood. She knew that Nabila was in a troubled marriage, and she welcomed her friend, hoping that a peaceful hour would restore her self-esteem. After giving her the dress, Zuha guided her to a chair by the fountain, then went back to her room. Watching the rebellious expression on Nabila's face, Zuha realized that the secret dresses were much more than a silly affectation.

A few days later, Zuha was returning from the market, when she found Yousef pounding on her door. Pleading for her help, he explained that Nabila had drunk stove cooking fuel and was convulsing.

People stood aside as Zuha raced by them. Yousef trailed behind. Upon her arrival, Zuha found found the seemingly lifeless body of her friend on the floor. She immediately began pressing her stomach and turning her body to make her vomit up the poisonous oil. Yousef stood by watching helplessly, as his young daughters Samira and Halima cried. Abandoning civility, Zuha shouted at Yousef to take the girls away. She lifted Nabila into a sitting position and stuck her finger down her throat. Nabila vomited, expelling everything in her stomach. Gasping for air, she opened her eyes and saw Zuha holding her. Still enraged, Zuha called Yousef and commanded him to mop the floors. He complied. She said that she was going to take Nabila to her own house, and until she was fully recovered, he would have to care for the girls. She packed fresh clothes and took her away.

Not accustomed to caring for his daughters, Yousef didn't know how to console them. His next-door neighbor, hearing their cries, finally took them to her home, cursing the uselessness of their father. Nabila was grateful to be with her friend, but felt uneasy about being away from her daughters. In the end, she felt too exhausted to resist the comfort of Zuha's bed and fell asleep.

The next morning, Zuha followed her usual morning ritual, putting her coffee on a tray and walking into her garden.

But her mind was still on Nabila. She knew that she would have to send her back home to her daughters. She also knew that Yousef's initial compliance was the result of shock, fearing that his wife was going to die. She was certain that he would soon come and demand his wife's return.

At that moment, Nabila came out and said that she was ready to return to her girls. Reluctantly, Zuha walked her back, but she was still worried for her safety, and feared that Nabila might try to take her life again.

Over the next few days, Zuha's mind continued to drift back to Nabila and her daughters, but she knew that she couldn't do much for her. She decided to take the afternoon off and went to look in on her. To her surprise, Nabila looked at peace with herself. Nabila explained that her husband had hidden the jerrycan containing the poisonous stove fuel. She interpreted his gesture as an act of love. Somewhat relieved, Zuha returned to her house. Since it was almost dusk, and too late to resume her sewing, she decided to remove her in-laws' personal possessions from the armoire. Going through their clothes, Zuha uncovered an old book of poetry tucked away between the folded garments. Realizing that it was written hundreds of years ago, Zuha sat on her bed and began to read a poem written by the Granadan poet Hafsa bint Al-Hajj. She was surprised to read the account of this Arab woman freely extolling the erotic pleasures that she had experienced with her lover, Abu Ja'far, the Andalusian poet. The poetry of Hafsa bint Al-Hajj and that of other female poets in the book were new to Zuha. As a young woman, she loved to write stories and poems, but her marriage had ended that practice.

Unable to keep up with the increased demands of her many clients, Zuha asked Nabila for help. It was a way to get Nabila out of her house, and she thought that some financial help might improve Nabila's relationship with her husband, yet the opposite was true. When Yousef found out that his wife was working, he showed up at Zuha's door in a rage. Again, he had difficulty expressing his anger in Zuha's serene presence. He listened to Zuha explain that Nabila could not have found a safer place to be: "Your wife is behind these high walls and I'll make sure that she goes home before the girls return from school. Nabila will also be making money. She could help you pay for some of the household expenses." Persuaded by the financial argument, Yousef departed quietly.

A week later, Nabila reported to Zuha that, by having extra money in his pocket, Yousef often left the house without his usual threats, and he was still pleasant when he returned at the end of the day. Happy with this sudden change, Nabila felt that perhaps his anger was circumstantial, and that in time he could change. However, it was not long before her husband returned to his aggressive behavior.

Nabila told Zuha that she would have left him long ago had her own father not sent her back when she returned home to ask her parents for help. "My father sided with him, accusing me of being a rebellious wife. He explained to me that a man has to vent his anger somewhere."

Seeing how distraught her friend was, Zuha took her outside to sit near the fountain. She could not find the right words to say. The only thing that she could offer her was her garden and the poetry book that she had found in the armoire, to take her mind off her troubles.

After working on her machine for a while, Zuha went back out to see how Nabila was, and found her completely immersed in the book. "I can hardly believe that there was a time when Arab women were allowed to express their love and lust freely without shame," she said. Happy to see that Nabila was calmer, Zuha made lunch and they spent the day reading to each other by the fountain.

Zuha was walking to the market one day, when she saw the book vendor anchoring a large umbrella into a base that he had fabricated out of a metal container filled with stones. Feeling a slight embarrassment at being caught without his jacket on, he apologized for his disheveled appearance. He was reassured when Zuha said that she liked the umbrella. Since she was already on the carpet, she selected a book and was about to pay for it, when he took it from her hand and placed it in a paper bag bearing his name. She looked at the bag and read aloud, "Mustafa Amin, Book Vendor." Beaming with pride, he thanked her and went back to finishing his work on the umbrella.

For the rest of the week, the image of Zuha's lips uttering his name continued to float in his head. He began to anticipate her return. The next few days, he was distracted and even curt with his female customers, whose only offense was that they were not Zuha, the woman he was longing to see.

Zuha and Nabila were sewing side by side when a new client came to the door. Surprised to see a woman with short hair and wearing pants like a man, they were reluctant to let her into the house. Speaking softly, she greeted the two women, apologized for wearing pants, then removed the white jacket that she wore on top of her tight-fitting blouse, revealing the contours of her small breasts. "This is all I have to offer as proof of my gender." Zuha smiled and let her into the courtyard.

Being a city woman, Rula was not only different in appearance, but her way of speaking was more direct. She looked at Zuha and asked, "What is a beautiful woman like you doing behind these walls?" Feeling defensive, Zuha said that it was where she wanted to be.

Fascinated by the new client, Nabila asked if she was there for a wedding dress. Rula laughed. "I don't have time for marriage." Nabila was dumbfounded. She had never imagined that a woman had a choice not to marry.

Rula explained that she wanted a traditional dress to wear to a special event. Zuha took her measurements, then offered her a cup of coffee. In the kitchen, Rula watched with fascination as Zuha made coffee, which needed to be boiled seven times. Zuha would lift the little pot every time it foamed and was about to boil over. When the foam settled down, she would put it back on the stove and boil it again. Rula asked why coffee had to be boiled seven times. Careful not to look away from the boiling coffee, Zuha said that it was what her mother had always done.

"My mother and every other mother in the country and their mothers always boiled it seven times too," answered Rula. "But we never did know why."

"Let's see what happens if we only boil it six times," said Zuha mischievously, and they walked out smiling.

Enchanted by the garden and the charming atmosphere, Rula sat near the fountain, slowly sipping her coffee, so slowly that day turned into twilight. Realizing that it was late, she thanked Zuha and left in a hurry.

A short time later, she returned. She had missed the last bus out of Baradi and didn't know what to do. Zuha offered her the guest room. As night approached, Zuha lowered the oil lamp from the ceiling, removed its glass chimney, lit the wick, and placed the chimney back on the lamp. She pulled on the string that was threaded through the pulley on the ceiling and lifted the lamp back to its desired height.

After dinner, she lit the portable lamp, so that she and her guest could move around the house. Rula watched as their shadows danced on the walls. Mesmerized, she waved her arms in the air and saw her shadow respond. Captivated, she broke into a full dance. Zuha looked on with delight as her guest abandoned decorum. At ease with her body, Rula danced freely.

Leading the way, Zuha walked out to her courtyard and sat by the fountain. The moonlit sky, overshadowing the oil lamp, made their shadows disappear. Rula sat panting and trying to catch her breath, before declaring that it was the most fun she had had in a long time.

It was six in the morning when the aroma of coffee reached Rula's room. She opened her eyes and was happy to see that the light had returned. Zuha was already outside by the fountain sipping her coffee. Rula quickly joined in. After breakfast, Zuha walked her to the bus stop and asked her to return in three days for her first fitting.

Zuha was walking back from the bus station when she spotted a man with his donkey standing in the middle of

Mustafa's carpet. Noticing her, Mustafa Amin stopped un-loading his books from the side-saddles. He quickly handed the owner of the animal a large bill for his service and asked him to leave. The man, surprised at the large amount, shouted his thanks and asked God to bestow blessings onto Mustafa, his generous client. This only served to draw more attention to the scene. Not wanting to disturb the two men, Zuha looked away, nodding to Mustafa only when she was near the carpet.

Mustafa had never imagined that she would be in the market so early in the morning. He was distraught at having been caught with the donkey on his carpet. Was that why she kept on walking and didn't stop to speak? He thought of clos-ing his business. He thought of how much nicer it would be to have a store where he could leave books on shelves protected from the elements, rather than using the big tarp that he kept on hand during the rainy season. He also wondered about the great Russian books translated into Arabic by the Palestinian scholar Khalil Baydas. He asked himself whether authors like Tolstoy would have approved of having their books sold on the street in the same way that cabbages were sold. Yet wasn't it true that a book's contents remained the same in any setting?

Feeling dejected, he went home earlier than usual. The smell of freshly baked bread in his mother's kitchen caused him to murmur a blessing for her hands. For most of his life, it had been a scent that made him feel secure. That day was no exception. His mother was an old woman who stayed at home and moved around her house doing what she could. She thanked God for granting her a good son. Nothing gave her more pleasure than sitting down to a meal with him. But on that particular day, her son seemed troubled and unsure about his work. He complained about the indignity of having to sell his books on the street. She remained silent until he had finished his food. Finally, she said, "Have you forgotten how your father used to sit in that same location where your carpet sits now, writing letters to the British authorities on behalf of farmers who couldn't write? Sometimes he did it for free when people couldn't pay. But he was always grateful for whatever they could give."

Mustafa could not look his mother in the eyes. He managed to acknowledge his late father's dignity and apologized to his mother for doubting the value of his work.

Zuha was hand-stitching in her usual spot by the fountain when Salim, her childhood friend from Zatoni, arrived at her door. He wore a grave expression on his face. Zuha knew immediately that something had happened to her mother. Still, she waited for his announcement. In a kind voice, Salim said that his wife went to look in on her neighbor as she had done every day, but there was no answer. She continued to knock throughout the morning. Finally, she decided to open the door, and found Zuha's mother's lifeless body in bed.

After packing a small suitcase, Zuha walked with Salim to the small station in Baradi and took the bus back to her village. Upon their arrival, Salim walked to his house, where the men attending the funeral gathered. Zuha joined the women who gathered in her mother's house.

Each neighboring house emanated its own sound. While the women expressed their grief for the death of a friend and neighbor through shrill wailing, Salim's house reverberated with the deep voices of men trying to give reasons for why we live and die. The chorus of voices echoed like sad music throughout the surrounding hills. The women's cries turned into sobs when four men walked into the room, picked up the coffin, and walked out, leading the procession to the cemetery.

For the rest of the week, Zuha received people in her mother's living room by day, while her nights were spent alone in shock. She asked herself how something as enormous as the death of her mother could arrive so casually, and without warning. Unable to come to a decision about what to do with her mother's house, Zuha locked the door and left the town of her birth, holding the key in her hand, her tight grip giving her comfort.

Although she had lived separately from her mother for many years, the finality of her death was more than she could bear. She cried for most of her journey back to Baradi. Unlocking the door to her courtyard, she walked across her garden, opened the second door that led to her living quarters, and sat at her sewing machine, comforted by the familiarity of the old machine's scent. Although it was a glorious day, she stayed inside. Mustafa came to her mind, and she wished that she could walk to his carpet and talk to him, but knew that she had to stay at home, for the news of her mother's death traveled quickly.

Many people came to offer condolences. Zuha found herself immersed in the formalities of grief, tending to its customs and rituals, repeating the same scripted language with every visitor. Strangely, she found solace in the artificiality of her composed self.

Mustafa was also thinking about Zuha. He spent the day anticipating his visit to her house. His mother, eager to pay her respects to Zuha, was already on the street waiting for him to escort her. Upon their arrival, Mustafa stood by the large door and took a deep breath, before pulling on the bell's rope, making sure to conceal his excitement and adopt the appropriate expression for the occasion. Zuha had expected most women who lived in Baradi to come to her house, but she didn't anticipate seeing Mustafa at her door. Comforted by his presence, she sat next to his mother and listened to her as she went through the customary laments formally required on such occasions. For the rest of the week, Zuha found herself thinking about Mustafa, and looking forward to the day when she could see him again.

Relieved to learn that her town's rules were lenient about the death of an old mother who had lived elsewhere, she resumed her work and her normal routine, which included stops at Mustafa's carpet. Having spent so much of his time thinking about Zuha, Mustafa decided to take a chance. He wrote a letter declaring his love for her.

The next time she came for a book, he discreetly placed his letter between the pages. At home, Zuha sat by the jasmine to read and was overjoyed when she discovered his plea for her heart. They began to express their love for one another in letters hidden in books whenever she visited his carpet. Unable to contain her joy, Zuha decided to tell her friend Nabila about Mustafa Amin's love letters. Curious, and wanting to take a closer look at him, Nabila stopped at his carpet after work and bought a book.

Nabila's husband was home alone one day when he decided to have a look at the books that had been occupying his wife's mind lately. She had been staying up late to read, and it had aroused his curiosity. Going through her novels, he came across the poetry book, lent to her by Zuha. Enraged by the erotically explicit poem by the Andalusian female poet I'timad Arrumaikiyya, he assumed that the book came from Mustafa's carpet. In the kitchen, he located a bottle of kerosene stored under the sink. He rushed to Mustafa Amin's carpet, determined to cleanse his town of the filth he believed was corrupting his wife.

With the bottle in hand, he approached the bookseller and began to pour kerosene on the carpet. Horrified, Mustafa tried to defend his books by pushing him away, but he was no match for the bigger man's bad temper. A brawl ensued. Yousef pulled a retractable knife from his pocket and stabbed Mustafa in the chest. He then threw a lit match onto the carpet, causing the kerosene to ignite with a loud thud.

People in the market came rushing to the scene. Crowds gathered around and pulled Mustafa away from the flames. The intense heat of the burning books drove people back. They could only stand and watch as charred flakes of burning pages sparkled as they floated upward. Responding to the commotion in their town, Zuha and Nabila rushed to the scene. The police were handcuffing Yousef who was still shouting obscenities at the lifeless body of Mustafa Amin.

Spotting Nabila out of the corner of his eye, Yousef shouted even harsher obscenities at her. To avoid a scandal, Zuha left quickly and walked back to her house where she could mourn Mustafa's death in private. A few good men in the market went to the fabric shop and asked for a piece of white linen cloth. They shrouded Mustafa Amin's body and carried him away. People began to gather by the burned carpet. Although the few supporters of Yousef's action were outnumbered, they were loud in their demands that all books be banned in their village. In an act of defiance, the young men and women who frequented Mustafa's carpet gathered at the site and, one by one, placed books on the scorched ground.

Without Mustafa's love and his books, Zuha's life felt empty. She spent most of her time thinking of the joy that his letters had brought her. She mourned her mother's and Mustafa's death all at once. After many days of mourning, she grew tired of her passive life, doing what others expected of her. Worried that Mustafa's death would be forgotten, she spent evenings thinking of ways to honor his memory.

After several months of trying to conceive of a way to commemorate his efforts to educate the villagers, she went to the mayor's office and asked for permission to build a small memorial to Mustafa and his books. Reluctant to give his permission, the mayor complained about how he had to have all municipal matters approved by the British representatives in Baradi. Zuha explained that what she was proposing to do was only a modest memorial and not a grand monument: "All I want to do is replace Mustafa's carpet with a tiled replica on the same spot where he used to stand, then place a bench for young people to gather and to exchange books."

Unable to resist such a good idea, the mayor gave in and granted her permission. After hiring men to pour the cement bed in preparation for the tile work, Zuha took them to the site, where the burn marks still outlined the carpet. When the cement work was finished, Zuha traveled all the way to

Hebron, where ceramic tile making had been a tradition for centuries, and commissioned a replica of Mustafa's carpet.

In April of 1936, the crates containing the decorative tiles arrived in Baradi. The excitement was intense when the tile setters began to place the tiles on the cement. Even the mayor made a visit to the site. When the work was completed, a wrought-iron bench was placed on the floor, beneath a large umbrella. Zuha took great pleasure in seeing the memorial completed. The beautiful tiles stood out, inviting people with their lush colors, and it was not long before young men and women were seen reading on the bench.

Nabila was working at the sewing machine when she heard the erratic sound of the brass bell, suggesting to her that an out-of-town visitor was on the other side of the door. Opening it, she startled the Englishman who was still pulling on the cord. He didn't let go of the rope until she asked him to stop. He nervously reached for a card in his shirt pocket and handed it to her. She was surprised when he spoke to her in Arabic. "My name is Richard," he said, "and I'm here on an assignment for a newspaper." After explaining that he was stationed in Haifa, he said that his paper in London had picked up a news item from one of the local papers in Palestine about the memorial in Baradi and decided to do their own story. He told Nabila that many people in London were intrigued by the memorial to books built by a woman and wanted to visit her town. Sensing that she was reluctant to let him in, he added, "The mayor was happy to hear that people were planning to come to Baradi. When I stopped at his office, he sanctioned my visit to see the woman who created the memorial."

Nabila said that Zuha was away and asked him to return a little later. Having walked for a long time in the hot sun, he asked if he could just wait in the garden. Seeing how tired he looked, she invited him in and motioned to the chair near the fountain. She returned to her sewing machine. Then, feeling rude for not being more hospitable, she decided to ignore the rules that forbid a woman from entertaining a man. She went to the kitchen and prepared lunch for him. After eating, Richard thanked her and offered to carry the dishes to the kitchen. Never having seen a man help with household tasks in her village, she grinned and let him do it.

The ease that Richard felt in Nabila's company was instantly wiped out when Zuha walked through the courtyard door. He stood up nervously trying to conjure the right words with a language that did not flow easily from his mouth. Having experienced so much grief, Zuha had to force out a smile to ease his discomfort. Richard smiled back and extended his hand, along with an apology for his reticent tongue. He explained the reason for his visit and asked if he could interview her at the memorial ground. She agreed. They walked over to the memorial, and Richard took a picture of her sitting on the bench.

In the fall of 1936, the first bus of English visitors arrived in Baradi. The mayor, filled with pride, wore his finest clothes and stood with his entourage, which included the British police chief, now stationed in the same office that used to be the official Turkish command post for northern Galilee. That same week, Nabila's husband Yousef was stabbed in his jail cell by a man who was described by the British authorities as "the mad poet." The paper reported that the incident occurred after the poet, who shared Yousef's jail cell, discovered that his cellmate was the killer of Mustafa the book vendor. Many readers, however, suspected that the story was fabricated and was simply an excuse to lock up the poet in prison for fear that his resistance poetry about the British rule in Palestine was inciting people to rebel against the British authority. The poet was, after all, a well-regarded man and not a killer. People also knew that British officials were aware that Yousef was a small sacrifice, and that few in Baradi would protest his death. Nabila and her two daughters, Samira and Halima, however, spent the night crying for a father they hardly knew and a family that never was.

Rain fell hard the day Yousef was put to rest, but every man in town came to pray for his soul and ask God to forgive his sins. No one spoke ill of him any longer. The rumored circumstances of his death at the hands of the British authorities seemed to annul his sins. He was even perceived by some to be a martyr. In spite of herself, Nabila was pleased with this outcome for the sake of her daughters. The whispers they heard at the schoolyard about their father being a killer stopped and were now replaced by sympathy.

Nothing had really changed in Nabila's life except for her title. She was now referred to as a widow, a designation that seemed to garner compassion and respect. For the first time, she felt truly liberated from her husband. Without the means to stay at home for the expected forty day mourning period, she made a decision to return to her work soon after people stopped coming to her house to offer their condolences.

The stillness of an early morning was interrupted by the distant sound of hooves approaching. A knock resonated from

Zuha's courtyard door. A donkey with saddlebags brimming with books stood next to the man who used to bring Mustafa Amin's novels to the carpet. Startled by the sight, Zuha glared at the man, who looked as if he was not expecting anyone to answer so early in the morning. He stood at her door, welcoming the new day by giving prayers of thanks and expressing his admiration for God's beautiful creation.

Finally addressing Zuha, he explained that Mrs. Amin had asked him to discreetly deliver these books to her. He apologized for the early delivery. Zuha opened the door all the way and let him and his donkey in. The two proceeded to unload the books from the saddles. The man said that he would be delivering more the next day at about the same time. He gave her a note from Mrs. Amin and left. In her note, Mustafa's mother explained that she was having difficulty reading the small print, and that she could not think of anyone more deserving of her late son's books. Some of them were brand new and were from his business stock. Others came from his private shelves. Zuha had not read a new book since Mustafa's death. It was a comfort to her to have something of his as a way of remembering him.

It was almost spring when the mayor announced that a second bus would soon be arriving in Baradi. He asked the merchants to spruce up their restaurants and shops in preparation for the English visitors. Excited about the prospect of prosperity, they began to scrub their stores and sweep the streets. Seeing that many people from neighboring towns and cities were also coming to Baradi to see the memorial, Abu Shanab, the butcher, the most ardent supporter of the

36

book ban in town, decided to give up his business. Although motivated by greed, he washed his bloodstained apron and replaced the small meat-trimming knife that he kept in the top pocket with a pen. He painted the walls and stocked his old butcher shop with books. In his zeal, Abu Shanab decided to stay behind after all the other merchants went home in order to make a banner. With the aid of an English dictionary, he wrote, "English people are welcome in Palestine," and strung it on the market gates.

When the baker and the vegetable vendors returned the next morning, they tore the sign off the gate. Abu Shanab arrived shortly after, and he was enraged by the sign's disappearance. He had wrongly assumed that investing hours painting a welcome sign on behalf of everyone would be appreciated. Indifferent to colonial rule, he wondered why anyone would sabotage his efforts. He began to intimidate the merchants by picking physical fights with anyone who tried to explain their point about the sign, which would be deemed offensive to the locals who shopped in the market. The harmony that had existed in Baradi ended when the British police were called to stop a fight between the merchants in the market. They rounded them up indiscriminately and took them away. After their investigation revealed the reason for the merchants' disagreement with Abu Shanab, the police released him and locked up the merchants who had rejected the sign, just to show them that they would not tolerate any dissent. An uneasy truce was established between the merchants and Abu Shanab. Tensions subsided when the bus arrived and tourists began to spend money.

Change had also begun to take place in the rest of the country, since Britain had been given a mandate by the League of Nations for Palestine. It was particularly the increased number of emigrants from Europe that truly began to change the atmosphere. Many languages could be heard on the streets of Baradi. Flush with money, some merchants began to praise the benevolence of their new rulers. But the mayor, having had closer dealings with the Mandate Authority, knew better. He never trusted Britain's "intentions" for Palestine. He also knew that the interest in the memorial would be short-lived, and that he would have to contend with the merchants' disappointment and anger when people lost interest and stopped coming to see it. But the mayor's authority had diminished. All he could do was watch as the real power in Baradi was given to a thug, who was openly colluding with the British police. The mayor was also forced to look on as Abu Shanab began to dictate to other merchants in the market. He knew that he couldn't go against the wishes of the British Authority. In fact, to make Abu Shanab's influence clear to others in the market, the British police chief gave him a handgun, which he wore in a holster under his shirt, though it was barely concealed.

Nabila stopped sending Samira to the market when she noticed that her daughter was turning into a lovely young girl. Although Samira was only thirteen and too young for marriage, it still bothered Nabila to think of the day when young men would come knocking on her door. But even at her young age, Samira had other plans. She modeled herself after her teacher, who had chosen education before marriage. Samira had the maturity of a much older person. Mademoiselle Awatef, her new French and English teacher, noticed her curiosity and good behavior. Still single at the age of thirty, Mademoiselle

Awatef had earned much sympathy from parents in Baradi. They treated her with the delicate kindness shown to terminally ill patients. But Samira admired her teacher's independence and confidence. Mademoiselle Awatef had come to northern Galilee from Haifa, where she had been orphaned at a young age. She ended up in a boarding school run by French nuns. When she graduated, the nuns decided to send her to a university in Paris, where she earned a degree in education. Mademoiselle Awatef could have stayed in Haifa upon her return from Paris. The city would have offered her greater opportunities, but she wanted to break away from the convent and start her life on her own terms, away from the nuns.

While reading the morning paper in her office in Haifa, Rula came across an article about the memorial in Baradi and a picture of Zuha sitting on a bench. Amazed, she read the story about the seamstress she still remembered fondly.

Rula worked for her father, who had prospered selling artifacts from the ruins of past empires in Palestine to English antique dealers who would sell them to museums and private collectors. Her father's rise to wealth and power was so rapid that rumors about their riches began to circulate. The locals imagined that the crates containing stone and glass objects that arrived at their house were filled with gold coins that Rula's father had uncovered from secret locations. It was not far from the truth: some of the trunks would not even have been able to hold the money that the objects were sold for.

Her father built a house for her, and one for each of her two brothers, on a large piece of land, which now formed a family compound where the entire family lived. Her home was filled with books and the latest European furniture, for although it was antiquity that had brought the family wealth, modernity was what she desired. Her garden, however, was scattered with ancient sculptures and stone tiles, which had once been the pathways leading to Roman temples, paved the path leading to her home.

Rula was perceived by the English antique dealers that came to do business with her as a woman of unusual strength. The dealers preferred to work with her father, who could more easily be persuaded to accept low offers for his artifacts. They were also uncomfortable with her choice of attire. Her passion for pants began when she first saw a photo of American women in a fashion magazine wearing pants and had commissioned a tailor to make a dozen pairs for her. In time, people began to call her "zalamie," which meant, "like a man," or, "possessed by a male spirit." Sheltered by her father's wealth, Rula continued to live by her own fashion standards, even as they violated the rules of her society. It was not long, however, before people began to hear about her generosity, and the financial help that poor families would receive from her if they needed to see a doctor or buy food for their children. Rula was happy to help, for she felt that the treasures that made her family rich belonged to everyone. Not wanting to upset her father, she remained obedient to him and concealed her inner conflicts about the nature of his business.

Rula was unique even in Haifa. She followed no conventions, and, in a society where everyone conformed, she did things her own way. Older women in her neighborhood were not comfortable with her, and some men began to blame her nonconformity to the education she had received from the

European schools in Haifa. Threatened by this new modern version of womanhood, men on the street lowered their eyes when she passed by and refused to look at her. The only one who didn't was the sweets seller. Rula was a regular customer in his store and bought boxes of sweets to feed her English clients as they did business over tea. Looking at her, the sweet seller would often say, "Miss Rula, while my sweets seem to go directly to a woman's hips, they appear to enter your spirit instead." Rula found his flattery amusing and rewarded him with generous tips, but he was sincere. Even when describing Rula to his wife, he would liken her delicate body and big brown eyes to a gazelle.

Noticing that his clients never dared to haggle with his daughter, Rula's father began to relinquish most of his responsibilities to her. He said, in reference to the stone sculptures that Rula sold, that she was the only one in his shop who was able to squeeze so much money out of stones. This kind of praise made Rula's mother nervous. She muttered a little prayer of protection for her daughter, asking God to shield her from evil eyes. She went to the market and bought a glass evil eye protector and hung it above Rula's door.

Of all her English clients, Rula liked John the most. He also worked for his father, who ran one of the biggest antique stores in London. He was close to Rula's age and always had a good story to tell. His business often took him to the various parts of the British empire in search of antiquities, and his ability to describe the places he visited was so poetic that he made her forget, if only briefly, the opposition that she and all Palestinians had toward British rule. She also felt that John did not have the superior colonial character of the other men that came to shop at her warehouse. His open mind allowed him to embrace other traditions, and he spoke fondly and with respect when describing the people and cultures that he had visited. Rula's short hair and pants never intimidated him. Sitting with her under the olive tree filled him with pleasure, and whenever she asked him to come in for lunch, he would tell her that he preferred nothing more than eating under the olive tree. Understanding the social constraints of her culture, he did not want to offend her family by going into her house without a chaperone.

Seeing how close Rula and her father were, and witnessing the praise and affection she received from him, John marveled at their relationship. His own family was reserved. A stiff slap on the back was all he could hope for after concluding a good business deal. Anxious to get as much as he could out of Palestine, John's father sent him to Rula's house repeatedly. John soon realized that he was deeply attracted to her. He proposed to her on more than one occasion, but Rula, thinking that he was simply being flirtatious, would always smile and dismiss his proposal with a shrug. She felt that even if he was sincere, people would not approve of her marrying an Englishman, and her family would be shunned. Still, she couldn't imagine life without his visits.

Rula was in John's office one day when she noticed another article in the English paper about the memorial in Baradi. Curious to see what the seamstress had done, she finally took a day off and traveled there. Delighted to see her, Zuha and Nabila stopped working and sat with Rula by the fountain, reminiscing about her last visit. Then they took her to the memorial. Seeing how different the small town looked since her last visit, Rula asked if people in Baradi were pleased with the sudden change that the memorial brought. Zuha said that the merchants were pleased with their economic success, but they complained that the memorial was no longer used by the locals. She said that it was more often occupied by English visitors and British soldiers from the nearby camp. Zuha explained that a group of local poets were trying to organize and raise funds for a national poetry festival to be held on the memorial ground as a way to reclaim it from the tourists. Inspired, Rula felt that the project was a worthy cause and offered her time and financial help to support the festival. During their lunch in the garden, Nabila asked Rula in a teasing way if a wedding dress was the reason for her visit this time. "Not yet," replied Rula with a smile, "but maybe soon." She went on to tell them both about the Englishman who had been proposing to her.

John stopped traveling when his father decided to open an office with a warehouse in Haifa. He entrusted his son with the task of looking for a suitable location near the harbor. John began to spend most of his free time with Rula in her garden. On one particular day, John's knocks on Rula's door were unanswered. He went to her parent's house and learned that she had temporarily moved to Baradi to help organize a poetry festival.

Meanwhile, Zuha's house had been transformed into an office, with volunteers writing notes to poets and asking them to attend. Wanting to be with Rula, John took the bus to Baradi every morning and spent the day at Zuha's house, not leaving until the last bus departed.

They were sitting alone by the fountain one day when John declared his love for her again. Rula knew the dangers of letting herself fall in love with an Englishman, but she told herself that he was different from the others. She moved closer and allowed John to kiss her for the first time.

On a beautiful summer day in 1937, the week-long poetry festival took place in Baradi. Poets came from as far away as Jerusalem. Many came from Nazareth. There was so much energy and excitement on the first day that it made the British police nervous. They kept their distance and allowed the event to happen on their watch. But when more people arrived on the second day, the police called for reinforcements. Panicked, they decided to call in the riot police. They circled the memorial from a distance, and then, observing that it was nothing but a peaceful cultural gathering, retreated while the poets recited poems of resistance to the British rule. Witnessing the riot police leave was a small victory for Zuha, and the festival proceeded without incident.

After Rula returned home, much of her spare time was spent with John at his newly rented flat near the harbor. Rooted in Haifa, John began to expand his business. He imported English antiques, which his father's company loaded onto the same boats that came to pick up what he had bought in Palestine. With more British citizens and businesses moving to Haifa, John found a new market for his father's company. He liked being in Haifa, and was always included when Rula's family celebrated an occasion. Her father enjoyed John's company and valued his business, while her mother was truly enamored with his gentle nature. Seeing how fond Rula and John were of

44

each other made her happy. She knew how scandalous it would be if her daughter married an Englishman, and secretly she wished that he would marry her daughter and take her away to London. She knew that local men were intimidated by Rula and would never have the courage to propose to her.

Pleased with the success of his business in Palestine, John's father decided to travel to Haifa. Nervous about his visit, John began organizing the warehouse during the daytime, and sat up until midnight, updating his business books. His biggest fear, however, was his father's reaction to his relationship with Rula. Upon his arrival in Haifa, the first thing the English businessman wanted to do was meet the man who had sold his son so many wonderful artifacts. Rula's father had also been eager to meet him, and an invitation for dinner was extended to the man from England.

Both men were in high spirits that day. The similarities between them was so striking that it was hard for John and Rula to believe that their respective fathers had come from different cultures. Both wore fine suits and had an exaggerated air of self-confidence. The gold watches on their wrists were exactly the same. Proud of his status as an antique dealer, Rula's father decided to show off his most precious objects, which he kept in a large glass cabinet in the living room. The most exquisite items in his collection were five Fayum mummy portraits, smuggled from Egypt at great risk. The portraits were the only thing in his house not for sale. They were used only to test the depth of his client's pockets. Huge sums of money were often offered as enticement for the portraits, but he always turned them down.

Although his father had been in Haifa for nearly a week, John had not yet found the courage to confess to him his love for Rula. This was, in part, because they had been spending their evenings at the Officers Club drinking with other English expats. In the end, John felt that he could not let his father leave before telling him that he was in love with Rula. After a few drinks one night, he simply blurted out the truth. His father tried to emphasize their cultural differences and asked his son to reconsider his feelings. It was one thing for him to have dinner with Rula's family, but having his son wed an Arab girl was out of the question. He set out to sabotage his son's plans.

Only a few days later, his father appeared at John's office with a young blonde woman named Ruth Zuckerman, a new émigré from Poland. He had been introduced to her by one of the senior officers in the club, and he offered her a job as his son's secretary. John tried to tell him that he had everything under control, but his father insisted, and he accepted Ruth as his secretary. Ruth was a beautiful and soft-spoken woman. Her blonde hair framed a set of big blue eyes on a pleasant face. Unable to find work for her, John began to look for projects just to keep her busy. He soon realized that having Ruth in the office made it easier for him to visit Rula more often.

Rula and Ruth quickly became friends, as they were a similar age and both enjoyed going for walks on the beach. Ruth began to visit Rula and, like John, she was invited whenever Rula and her family celebrated an occasion. But John began to spend more time at the Officers Club. If a week went by without him showing up, his father would somehow find out and send him a reminder, telling him that it was his civic duty to socialize with the young men who were far away from home serving their country. Fearing that his father would find out, John never had the courage to ask Rula to accompany him to the club. However, Ruth was always at the club in the evenings, and John found himself spending hours in her company. After a while, Ruth began to ask him to walk her home from the club, which was often after midnight.

Rula, on the other hand, was spending her evenings answering letters received from groups seeking her financial help. They had heard about her involvement with the festival in Baradi. Her father, seeing an opportunity to polish his tarnished name with a community that was resisting colonial rule in Palestine, and nervous about his own close ties with British nationals, began to contribute large sums of money to his daughter's fund, of which Rula used a portion to advance women's causes in Jerusalem. Rula soon accepted an invitation from the women there and spent a week in Jerusalem, getting to know others who shared her independent lifestyle. Although she found the experience life-affirming, she missed John dearly and was eager to return to Haifa so she could share her experiences with him.

Upon her arrival, Rula dropped off her suitcase at her house and went straight to his flat. But he was not there. Disappointed, she returned to her house and found a note from him in the mailbox telling her that he was in London. Hoping to find more information about his sudden return, she went to see Ruth. She was not at home.

It was not until John returned that Rula learned his father had asked him and Ruth to travel to London. He had also given the power of attorney for his business in Haifa to Ruth Zuckerman, just in case John had to return to England. Saddened by the news of his possible departure at any moment, Rula spent most of that day with him in his flat. She could sense that John was nervous and cold. He couldn't tell her what would happen to their relationship if he were summoned back to London. Back in her garden, Rula sat under the olive tree, surrounded by kneeling Roman stone soldiers who, at a moment's notice, she could ship out of Palestine. Sitting there, she reflected on John's sudden change of attitude. It seemed as if he was already mentally preparing for his exit from Haifa.

When a week went by without hearing from him, Rula was so worried that she decided to visit John's office. Surprised to see that it was closed in the midafternoon, she went to his flat and found him in bed with Ruth Zuckerman. She felt such anger at his betrayal that she slammed the door and left without saying a word. Deeply hurt but proud nonetheless, Rula was determined to never see John again. Sitting in her living room, all she could think of was Zuha and the other village women that she'd met while helping to arrange their poetry festival. Knowing how difficult it would be if she continued to work with her father, Rula packed a small suitcase and took the bus to Baradi, hoping she could heal her broken heart in the comforting presence of Zuha and the other women.

Exhausted after a hard day at work, men sat slumped in their seats. One by one, they began to close their eyes as the bus left the station in Haifa. Fatigue and the motion of the moving bus lulled everyone to sleep, except for the man sitting next to Rula. He felt it would be impolite to surrender to sleep in the presence of the young woman next to him, and he took it upon himself to keep her company. Looking at her short hair and neatly pressed pants, he assumed that she was a visitor to Palestine and addressed her in English. He had learned to speak it at the refinery, built by a British oil company close to Haifa where he worked. The man was surprised when Rula replied in Arabic. Although she was not in the mood for small talk, she decided to be gracious and listen as he described the pipeline that brought oil all the way from Kirkuk, in Iraq, to the refinery in Haifa.

The smell of wild thyme in the air caused the man to lean his head closer to the window. He took a deep breath. Enticed by the scent, Rula also moved closer to the window and drew a breath. She leaned back in her seat, comforted by the presence of the man sitting next to her. But the man suddenly appeared to be taken over by melancholy. He explained that he felt guilty every time he took a deep breath of sweet air. He told her about his friend who fell into a holding tank at the refinery and drowned in oil. As if talking to himself, the man looked away: "The supervisor at the refinery deposited a few English pounds into the coffin. I was assigned to accompany the English pickup driver to deliver my dead friend to his wife."

For the rest of the way the man sat still and stared at the receding hills as the bus sped toward Baradi. Although she was still deep in her own sadness, Rula found kind words to offer the man sitting next to her. She felt a strange kind of relief that she would not be marrying an Englishman.

Zuha was watering her garden when Rula arrived. Rula asked if she could stay in the spare room for a while. After welcoming her with a big embrace, Zuha took her to her room and assured her that she could stay for as long as she wanted.

For several days, Rula kept to herself, but after a week she began to smile again. Zuha's steady and strong temperament, combined with Nabila's kindness and affection, soon lifted her spirits. She began to regard John as a chapter in her life that had to be closed. Unaccustomed to being idle, she did work around the house and prepared lunch for Zuha and Nabila as they worked on their sewing machines. She went to the market to shop for food and helped in the garden after sunset. There, she quickly learned that Zuha preferred silence as she tended to her flowers. In the evenings, they took turns reading poetry to one another with the oil lamp held close to the page.

Rula was walking back from the market when she noticed a young British soldier from the nearby camp sitting with his blonde girlfriend on the memorial tiles. He was being urged by the girl, who looked a little like Ruth Zuckerman, to use his bayonet to pry away a tile as a memento to their time together in Baradi. Dismayed, Rula tried to stop him, but he laughed and waved his bayonet at her. Alarmed by his behavior, Rula walked away, fearing that his action would invite others to do the same. When Zuha heard about the desecration of her memorial to Mustafa and his books, she went directly to see the mayor. After complaining to the police chief, the mayor was promised that the incident "would be investigated." But only a few weeks later another tile went missing, and then another.

Unable to convince the British police to take action, Zuha decided to take action herself, and enlisted Nabila and Rula, along with various friends who had been her customers over the years, to help her. To ward soldiers off of the memorial, they took turns sitting on the bench with books on their laps. Sometimes they read poetry to each other, and often they were joined by other women who felt it was a safe place to be. Even as more tiles vanished during the night, the significance of the memorial was not diminished. In fact, it increased over time. It became the place where people came together in Baradi to recite resistance poetry.

Eventually Zuha returned to her work and her garden, knowing that the memorial had its own life span and future. In her summer dress, happily working in the garden with Rula wearing pants by her side, Zuha reflected on how difficult and daring it must have been for Rula to adopt a new fashion so different from what every other woman in her society wore. Her relationship with Rula inspired her to take bolder steps. She stopped wearing her black mourning dresses and embraced cheerful colors, even outside her walls. Revisiting the idea of having a sign on her door, and aware that everyone in Baradi knew where she lived and could find their way to her house, she still wanted to claim her rightful identity openly. She didn't want to feel the shame she had experienced the first time that she dared to imagine naming herself as an individual without a husband. She took extreme care making her sign, sanding the small piece of wood smooth, and with a steady hand, she painted "Zuha's Dressmaking Shop" on it.

Nabila and Rula stood there and watched as Zuha hung the sign on her door. Nabila knew that she could never do what Zuha and Rula had done with their lives. But she hoped—and believed—that in time, her daughters would change what, for so many years, had seemed normal to women in Baradi.

THE ENGLISH GRAMOPHONE

The funerary bells were always a welcome sound in my all-boys primary school, which sat next to the church that my mother and father, and the rest of our family in Nazareth, attended. Gleeful for the opportunity presented by a death, we would run whenever we were summoned by the schoolmaster to pray for the dead. Since we were too young to affect the world around us, we moved through our lives observing tragedies that were well beyond our imagination or control. We were the new spectators: still untouched by adult realities. We assumed that all events, joyous or catastrophic, unfolded for our entertainment and benefit. The dead man in the coffin was of no concern to us. Our goal was not to help send him to heaven. We were there for the cones of boiled wheat berries, mixed with raisins and walnuts, and covered with sugar cubes, that were offered by the family of the deceased in exchange for our prayers.

As instructed by our superstitious parents, we avoided our customary path home after attending funerals, fearing that the angel of death was still close by and could discover the path to our doors. My friend Asad, who lived across from my house, and I would elude the angel by choosing the most complicated route home. We even offered the younger boys sugar cubes if they agreed to follow behind us and smooth our footprints.

My grandmother had a much deeper interest in the dead man. She wanted to know if he was young or old. I could tell that she was trying to measure her own life span against his. I had no idea, but I told her that he was very old. She crossed herself in relief, then said a prayer before accepting the sugar cube I had saved for her.

We lived in my grandmother's house. She had her own room that she had chosen herself. It was not the best room, but it had its own entrance that her friends used whenever they visited her. It was in that room that I learned the art of listening without appearing to pay attention to what was being said. I would feign interest in my grandmother's kitchen utensils, stacking forks and spoons on the little table in the far corner of her room. I once made a sunburst with forks just to convince my grandmother and her guests that I was engrossed in my task. As time went by, they stopped speaking in hushed tones, even when talking about sexual matters. I would repeat such details in the schoolyard in order to gain rank among the older kids in my class.

Of all my grandmother's friends, I was most interested in a younger one named Dalal, who lived next door. I always listened to her carefully. She was also the only woman in the room who referred to herself by name. She would often say things like, "Dalal was not born yesterday," and, "Dalal knows what the world is made of." It was as if her name was a separate entity that had privileges she herself did not have. Although the Arabic language designates other options for most words, Dalal always preferred naughty alternatives when talking about sex.

My grandmother was not old, but she was the wisest woman I knew. While many of her friends were more acquainted with other towns and cities, she gained her wisdom in the solitude of her room, surrounded by books that once belonged to her husband, who had taught her how to read.

I loved being with my mother also, but she always wanted me to shake hands with her visitors, who would then compare me to their own children. Since my mother was not the boastful type, I would end up looking tame in comparison to the other children, who seemed to be able to do so much more than I could. In my grandmother's room, the conversation with other women was rarely about their sons and daughters. It seemed to me as if they didn't care whether their offspring were a source of pride or shame. Unlike the younger women, who desired nothing less than the most noble human qualities for their children, the older women had learned that their sons and daughters were capable of possessing both.

My friend Asad was more daring than me. I always felt that it was because of his name, which meant "lion." My own name, Aqil, meant "the wise one" in classical Arabic, but the kids at my school called me Akel, which meant "the quiet" or "the timid one." I didn't like my name, and I often repeated what I'd heard from Dalal in the playground in order to prove that my name was not a correct representation of who I was. Still, I was Asad's equal when we played soccer with our improvised soccer ball made of rags from clothes we had outgrown. Since Asad's mother favored bright colors, we always saved his clothes for the outer layer.

I stopped craving sweetened wheat berries when Asad's father died and we had to pray for him. And although the cones were offered, I gave mine to the meanest bully in the playground, hoping to enter his good graces. But since he knew that he could have taken it away from me if he wanted to, he continued to taunt me.

The death of Asad's father made me aware of what the death of a father can do to a family. I began to pray more sincerely when our class was asked to join in funeral prayers. I never ate sweetened berries again. I developed an intense interest in my father, who seemed pleased by my thoughtfulness. He began to take me with him whenever he went to the market. I liked spending time with him but hoped that someday he would stop instructing me and just talk to me or show me his affection.

My grandmother's affection was boundless. It could be earned with ease. I never felt insecure in her company. All I had to do was show up and she would shower me with love. Her stories were my favorite. I loved the invisible worlds she conjured in her dim room. Her fairy tales were so vivid that they overshadowed what I had seen with my own eyes. I often wondered about my grandfather's whereabouts, but I never dared to ask her about him. Whenever I asked my mother about him, all I ever received was a reprimand. It was something that I thought about for a long while, as I saw that the world provided two grandparents for every other child in my neighborhood. Since my question provoked discomfort, my grandfather's absence became a mystery that fed my imagination with such abundance that I imagined him as all sorts of different characters. On good days, he would die in battles like the heroes my grandmother described in her stories. On other days, he would be a thief or a coward, hiding in shame in some forgotten cave.

I stopped spending so much time in my grandmother's room when a new boy named Saleh joined us in the middle of the school year. It took only a few days for us to become friends. Saleh never stayed at school for lunch. His family's bakery was so close that we could smell the delicious sweets baking in the oven while we ate in the in the lunch room. I was so excited when one day Saleh asked if I wanted to see the bakery after school. Stepping into the bakery, we were greeted by his father, who was at the sales counter. At the back of the store, a stone oven glowing with red embers was surrounded by shelves stacked with bread and sweets. This was where his mother worked. Pleased that her son had made a friend so quickly, she asked us to sit at the end of her bread table where she was working and served each of us a plate stacked with sweets. After we finished eating, Saleh said that he had to look after the front desk while his father went to the mosque for prayers. I was sent home with a small box of sweets.

Our teacher announced that the school had just acquired a movie projector. We, along with our families, were invited to attend the screening of *La Vie Merveilleuse de Bernadette*. My mother and father put on their finest clothes. We walked to the school accompanied by my grandmother and her friend Dalal. We took our seats in the auditorium, where chairs had been placed in rows facing a big white canvas. Everyone was mesmerized by the film. Our parish priest walked around with the expression of someone who was finally vindicated

57

and could offer proof of the power of faith that he had been preaching all these years. Cheering erupted when the Virgin Mary appeared to young Bernadette. This went on until the movie was finished and the lights came on. Startled by the sudden brightness, some people covered their faces. Before anyone could move, a group of ushers appeared and began to pass around the collection trays, urging people to reach into their pockets for any money they could spare.

On the way home, it was Dalal who spoke first. She protested the sudden onslaught of the ushers. Still entranced by the event, however, everyone looked at her disapprovingly. She had to bear the burden of her ill-spoken words all the way home down a street where, many years ago, the Virgin Mary had once walked. As if not able to separate fiction from reality, my grandmother said, "Our lady is even more beautiful than I had imagined." For the rest of the week, she only talked about the movie.

After a short while, Dalal, the most outspoken woman in my grandmother's group, grew tired of the topic. She stopped coming to our house, and I lost interest in my grandmother's room. I spent many hours at Saleh's store instead, doing homework after school and helping out with his chores. My other friend, Asad, the only remaining male at home after the death of his father, had too many responsibilities, and never came out to play. Although he was only ten years old, with two older sisters, his paternal uncles had come to prepare him for the role of man of the house.

The school year seemed to go on forever, and I was glad when it finally ended. My father took my mother and I away for the summer to a railroad car that had been converted into a small cottage. This is where my father lived during the week and only came home on his day off. It belonged to his English employer. The old train car had been moved to the beach in Haifa. My mother didn't like being there. The beautiful sea and the sound of waves breaking on the shore of the Mediterranean were not compensation enough for her to leave Nazareth and all her friends behind. She was also nervous about us being the only ones on the beach at night. Unlike her, I was able to put my faith in my father's hands. I always felt safe when he was around.

During the day, my mother and I sat outside under the makeshift canopy and watched the bathers. I never went into the sea when my father was at work because my mother couldn't swim. The water made her nervous, and she made me stay under the tarp.

She was inside making lunch one day when a boy and his mother walked by, their white skin and golden hair making them appear different from everyone else on the beach. I ran inside to alert my mother, but she seemed less surprised than me. She told me they were Templers from the German colony in Haifa. Since Templers was not an Arabic word, I didn't know what she meant. When my father came home, I asked him about the Templers. "They are a religious order from Germany," he told me. "Not to be confused with the ancient Knight Templars." Since I didn't know what my father was talking about, I simply decided to forget the whole thing.

The next day, I was flying a red kite that my father had made for me the night before, when the boy and his mother reappeared on the beach. Curious, the boy came over, and I let him hold the string of my kite. Even without a shared language, the boy and I became friends. We spent hours playing together. Envious of our ease, our mothers smiled awkwardly at each other as we ran through the shallow water. The boy and I met every afternoon, happy to be in one another's company. I stopped thinking about my return to Nazareth.

My father often went for a swim after work, and I swam in the shallow water. My mother and I would watch as he disappeared from our sight. One evening, I asked my father if he was ever scared to be out in such deep water. Only once, he told me, when he was trapped in a whirlpool and couldn't swim out. He had to invoke Saint Elijah, whose shrine loomed in the distance on top of Mount Carmel. The saint had answered his prayers and pulled him back to shore. That night, I lay under my bedcovers and prayed to Saint Elijah, thanking him for saving my father.

By the end of the month, the hot sun of Haifa, as though incensed by the blonde boy's insubordination, baked him to a color that matched my own. Without speaking, the boy and I still managed to have fun. We played and built sandcastles and flew the kite. There was never cause for disagreement. We followed one another happily. In time, however, I began to understand the limits of our wordless relationship. I could never tell him a joke, or describe Saleh's store, or the amazing sweets that his mother baked in the beautiful wood-burning oven. That said, I missed the blonde boy after we returned to Nazareth.

My grandmother was happy to see me, and I could tell that she had finally returned to herself. The spell cast on her by *La Vie Merveilleuse de Bernadette* had been broken. She was released from the burden of having to uphold the high virtues that religion demanded. Dalal had returned, and laughter was heard in my grandmother's room again.

Although my grandmother went back to telling her stories, it was not long before modernity seemed to be threatening to silence her again. My father bought a shortwave radio that told stories all day long. The radio became our most prized possession. It sat high up on a shelf, covered with an embroidered linen cloth. Neighbors came to see and listen to the radio. No one spoke a word. We sat solemnly around the shelf and listened.

It was strange not to see my father every day. I became used to being with him at night at the train car. Having my grandmother around was nice too, but she never failed to remind us of the sacrifice that her son was making for our sake. I often wished that we had a store full of foods and sweets like Saleh. His parents were together day and night, and they seemed to have all that they needed right there on their shelves. Sometimes, when my friend Asad missed his father and was sad, I pretended that my own father was dead too, especially when he was busy and didn't come home on his day off.

I was never sure if my mother was a stoic woman or just indifferent to my father's absence. She was the same when he was at home as when he was away. She was angry with him for buying the radio that attracted the neighbors to our house. One day, my father came home to find that the radio had been unplugged. She asked him to take it to his railroad car. Thinking that it was a kind gesture on her part, he explained to her that he was fine without a radio and that he liked his solitude. But my mother insisted. She said that she could no longer entertain people all day long and serve them coffee that we couldn't afford.

Without the radio, our life returned to normal. I was as pleased as my mother, although I wished we still had it when Saleh came to visit our home for the first time.

My life changed abruptly when my father decided to move us to Haifa. My mother and grandmother were not thrilled with the idea, but he had made his decision, and we had no choice but to follow him to a rented house near the German colony. I was sad to leave my friends, but also excited about moving to a city by the sea. United by their shared mutiny, my mother, who often kept her distance, finally achieved a fragile harmony with my grandmother. Together, they gave my father the cold shoulder. As a result, I spent more time with him on the beach. He truly loved the sea and always swam the farthest from the shore. I followed him with my eyes as far as I could, wondering what lay beyond the sea. The excitement that I felt about being with him every day of the week was more wonderful than anything I could have imagined.

Hoping to discover my new neighborhood, I ventured into the German colony to look for the Templers boy, but I couldn't find him. Nearly everyone around us spoke English or German. My father's English employer had helped him find the house. The indigenous people who spoke Arabic lived in the old part of Haifa, which was close by, but I never had the courage to walk on my own through a street that was patrolled by English soldiers armed with guns.

Classes at my new school in Haifa started soon after the lifeguard post was removed from the beach and was replaced by a sign that read "Swim at Your Own Risk." My new school was large, and the pecking order was already established. Being the new kid, I was often excluded from the group. Even after two months, I still couldn't make friends. I missed playing soccer with the rag football that Asad and I had made. While walking home one day, I came across the boy from the Templers colony and his friends. He was happy to see me and introduced me to everyone. One by one, they came to shake my hand. It felt strange to be shaking hands with other kids, but I assumed that it was part of their culture. I was always glad when I met them on the street. Other times, when I couldn't find him, I would walk to the foothill of Mount Carmel, where I spent hours roaming the mountain and gazing at Saint Elijah's shrine in the distance. My mother referred to that place as "Stella Maris." There were so many languages spoken in our country. New words began to seep into our own speech, but I never understood their meaning.

My friends were never far from my thoughts. I was separated from them by only thirty-five kilometers, but that seemed an enormous distance in those days. My grandmother's isolation was more severe. Without her friends' lively conversations, she became withdrawn and depressed. She tried to keep herself busy with household chores. Life felt tedious to all of us, except for my father, who was wholly focused on providing for us.

One day, I asked my grandmother if she would like to go for walk with me. She said yes right away. Having her by my side, I felt brave when we walked by the British soldiers, who stared at us as if we were the intruders and they were the inhabitants of Palestine.

When we returned home, my father and his English employer were sitting in the living room waiting for us. The man greeted me warmly but paid more attention to my grandmother. Although she could not speak English, he continued to talk to her. A little later, he asked if he could see our kitchen. Then he asked to see the washroom. It was an unusual request, because he didn't use the washroom. It looked as though he was just inspecting our hygiene standards. When my mother invited him to dinner, he smiled and accepted. When we were finished eating, he sat next to my grandmother and asked through my father if she would be willing to care for his young child during the day. She agreed.

The next day, the man came back with his wife and son, whom they introduced as Edmund. After sitting with us for a while, they said goodbye to their son and left. It didn't take long for Edmund to smile when I made a funny face for his amusement. My mother and grandmother fussed over him. Suddenly, the atmosphere in our house was transformed by Edmund's presence.

Seeing how happy her son was, the woman began to shower my grandmother with small gifts. She shared them with my mother. At the end of the month, she received an envelope containing her wages. She had never earned money before. Having her own money was significant. She began to feel different about her position in the house. She spent some of her money on a new shirt for me and bibs for Edmund. Suspecting that he was named after General Edmund Allenby, who led the conquest of Palestine, she always used the French version of his name, Edmond. After five months, her happiness was interrupted. Edmund's mother decided that he was ready to be in the daycare with other English boys. His departure affected my grandmother deeply.

I was also saddened by his departure. I enjoyed entertaining him after school. Seeing how unhappy I was, my grandmother, with all the money left in her purse, bought bus tickets to Nazareth for the two of us. My grandmother stayed with her friend Dalal, and I went to stay with Saleh and his family. Although our stay in Nazareth was brief, it reminded us that we still had friends, but all I felt was sadness. When it was time for us to leave, my grandmother wrote our address in Haifa on a piece of paper and invited Dalal to our house. Dalal folded the paper carefully and placed it in her jewelry box.

We were surprised to see Edmund at our house when we returned to Haifa. His parents had a meeting at the officer's club and asked my mother to care for him for few hours. Two weeks later, his father approached mine and explained that his son was not happy at the daycare. He asked if my grandmother would consider taking him back. One month later, to my grandmother's delight, Edmond spoke his first sentence in Arabic. He was a bright boy. In a short time, he was able to convey to her all his simple needs in her language. His mother was amused at first, but after a while, I saw the strain on her face when he began to speak to his own mother in Arabic. She stopped smiling and always took her son away from us in great haste at the end of the day. As time passed, I could see that she was not happy. She was beginning to see my grandmother's love for her son as vengeance against her, as well as the very empire that she was trying to nurture through her volunteer work at the officer's club. A few months later, she stopped bringing Edmund to our house and I never saw him again.

One day in 1936, my grandmother answered a knock on our door, never imagining that the man on the other side would be her husband, who had been assumed dead. Although it was clear that she recognized him immediately, the rest of us stood by and wondered who the man was. At sixty-six, he looked more like a man in his eighties. His white hair framed a face worn down to the bones. His head sat on a body that was as tired-looking as his face. Letting him in, she took him by the hand and introduced him to us. After resting for a while, he explained that he had spent years walking from Ankara in Turkey, and had finally inched his way back to Palestine. He said that he walked through Syria and made his way back to Nazareth, only to be told by Dalal that we had moved to Haifa. Dalal gave him our address and a bus ticket.

Since he was exhausted, we all went to bed early. I woke up to the faint sound of conversation between my mother and grandmother, who was lamenting her husband's physical decline. My grandfather's presence was hardly noticeable. He lay on my bed, which I had to relinquish, and it seemed to me that in all those years of walking, he had only been trying to make it home and find a bed to die in.

On the days that followed, he barely ate and never explained his long absence. I continued to listen to my grandmother's conversations, as I used to do when we lived in Nazareth. I looked intently at my open books, or drew pictures while sitting at the kitchen table, where all conversations took place. I learned that my grandfather had been a high-ranking officer in the Ottoman army, a rank achieved not by his ability to fire a gun, but by the skill of his pen. He had been a schoolteacher when the Ottomans drafted him, and he was taken to the Sinai desert. In an infantry where few men could read or write, he was a great asset. Being an officer meant that he had to flee with his soldiers when Britain defeated the Ottomans in the Sinai, and he ended up in Ankara.

While walking with my father one day, I asked him why my grandfather didn't speak to anyone or tell his stories. "Because his stories would reek of death," my father replied, with a tinge of anger in his voice. Afraid to say anything else, I wondered what death smelled like.

I developed a morbid curiosity about my grandfather and continued to eavesdrop on my grandmother's private conversations.

"For all these years," she said to my mother, "I have lived in anticipation of seeing the man that I loved. But now I don't seem to have any feelings for him. Although my curiosity is satisfied, as I desperately wanted to know where he was, seeing him motionless in bed is a constant reminder that he has not yet truly returned."

Because he was so exhausted, my grandmother had to feed him and keep him clean. Since I didn't have another bed to sleep in, I shared hers. She never liked it when I said something negative about my grandfather. I think that she was still in love with the memories of the life they had shared. My father rarely entered the room where his father slept, except when he had to help change him into clean pajamas.

My grandfather had arrived at our house with only the clothes on his back and a cloth bundle, which he placed

under the bed when he first arrived, and where he continued to sleep. We were all at home when my grandmother
decided to bring the bundle into the living room while he
slept. Untying the knot, she removed a few shirts and found
a cloth bag tucked carefully under them. Wanting to see
what was inside it, she loosened the string, then deposited
its contents onto the rug. We all watched as hundreds of
gold wedding bands rolled out in different directions on the
tiled floor. Alarmed, she swept the rings into a pile and put
them back in the bag. Speechless, we stared at one another.
My father estimated that there were nearly a thousand rings
in the bag. My grandmother anxiously took the bundle back
and placed it back under her husband's bed.

The next morning, as my father and I were walking to
school, he said, "You can never say anything to anyone about
the rings." I already knew that it was a secret, and felt hurt by
the tone in his voice.

My school was one of several schools in Palestine run by
Lasallian Missionaries. Like any other morning, we began
the day with prayers and continued with religious studies,
touching on the attributes of God, his love, wisdom, and so on.
Gradually, the stories would turn into tales of vengeance and
dire threats for anyone who didn't obey God's commandments.
I was not interested in my teacher's religious lessons and stories on that day, and I drifted back into my own thoughts.

Upset about my lack of attention, my teacher ordered me
to his desk, and I was punished with the cane. He did not stop
even after my hand turned red and began to swell. Unable to
endure the excruciating pain, I lowered my hand and refused

to extend it again. Enraged, he hit my arm. Without thinking, I seized the cane from his hand and threw it on the floor. Angered by my disobedience, he sent me to the principal's office. I was expelled from school.

My father blamed me for the expulsion, but my grandmother took a different position. She crossed herself and exclaimed, "These teachers are nothing more than foot soldiers for the new invaders." Although French missionaries ran my school, my grandmother was suspicious of anyone who set up institutions in Palestine. The verbal disagreement between my father and his mother became so deafening that my mother came out of the kitchen to hush their conversation for the sake of the sleeping man. However, it looked as though it was the very thing that he needed. He opened the door and came out waving his arms, acting as if he was trying to make peace between warring factions. Taken aback by his sudden resuscitation and authority, everyone stopped talking. He stood firm, as though his military rank had been restored.

My father went to the market with a list in his hand while my mother and grandmother began preparations for a special meal to celebrate my grandfather's recovery. After they were satisfied with their meal, my grandparents sat on the couch and talked. Upon discovering the reason for my grandmother's quarrel with their son, my grandfather moved a small table and two chairs to my old room, and I resumed my schooling with him as my teacher. In time, my grandmother and I began to take him for walks in the afternoon, and sometimes we took him to the market. He looked so harmless that we walked through a street full of British soldiers without fear of him being identified as an ex-Turkish officer.

Without friends, my mother and grandmother followed the same ritual, which seemed to be the only thing that gave them purpose. Every morning, they opened the windows to let in the fresh air, even if it was cold outside. They swept and mopped the already-clean floors, while my grandfather and I sat confined to his bed until the floors were dry. My grandmother tried to be civil when talking to her husband, but her anger about his long and unexplained absence often boiled over, especially when she was in the kitchen with my mother. There, I often heard her say, "Surely he could not have been walking for all those years. Something must have happened to him in between." But I enjoyed being with him, because his life was a mystery and he kept much of his past hidden.

Walking with him to the market one day, I noticed a wedding band on his finger that I had not seen before. When we entered the pastry shop, he took the ring off his hand and offered it in exchange for sweets. Thinking that he was a fool, the man quickly took the gold ring and gave me my treat. It seemed to me that my grandfather had done this with food merchants many times before. On the way home, I decided to ask about the rings under his bed. Surprised, he looked at me and then began to explain that he was an officer in the Turkish army. I told him that I already knew that from my grandmother. Without a pause, he continued, and told me he was in charge of collecting his fallen soldiers' tags, along with their wedding bands. Being an officer, he explained, meant that he had to march out with the rest of the surviving soldiers after the defeat of the Ottoman army in the Sinai. Upon his arrival in Turkey, the Ottoman soldiers under his command went to their own families. Since Turkey was in disarray, my grandfather decided to make his way back to Palestine. Since he didn't know anyone there, he was left to fend for himself. He kept the rings, which were supposed to be returned to his superiors, for his own survival. His story put me at ease, because I imagined that he had killed all the people to whom the rings belonged.

My father didn't spend much time with me anymore. I couldn't tell whether it was because he was busy, or because he wanted to offer his father a second chance at fatherhood. After a while, I became the only one who kept my grandfather company. I couldn't understand why my grandmother wasn't trying to make amends with him. It seemed unfair to me that I should be the only one responsible for his well-being. I even asked her to spend more time with him, but she said that she was no longer sure if he was the same man anymore. "There is nothing left in him that I recognize," she explained. "He is old and feeble and never bothers to explain his long absence to me."

I soon realized that I couldn't influence what she thought of her husband. With my schoolbooks in a satchel, my grandfather and I began to venture farther away from the house in order to explore different settings for my schooling with him. I worried about him and feared that he would never be part of our family.

In time, however, and with proper nourishment, he began to look well, and his personality began to change. My grandmother also noticed, and I could see her looking at him with renewed interest. After a few weeks, he pawned some of his rings with a jeweler in Haifa and bought a new suit. He hung it on a hook in his room. Everyone in the house noticed it, and they began to wonder what he was planning.

We were walking to the market one day when my grandfather said that he was going to move back to his house in Nazareth. I asked if I could go with him, but he told me that a child belonged with his parents. When he finally told the rest of the family, my exasperated grandmother said, "There's nothing in that house. We brought everything here. You'll have no mattress to sleep on." He explained that he had slept without a mattress many times before. When I asked him about my schooling, he said that it wouldn't be long before everyone would follow him, and we would all be together again. When it was time for him to leave, my grandmother told him that she couldn't let him go back on his own to a house that had been closed for so long, and that she would go with him. I didn't know if she was motivated by a sense of duty, or if my grandfather had earned her respect. A few days later, they packed a single suitcase and left.

My mother and I spent much of our time at home. I returned to my room. Without my grandparents, I felt lonely, but never complained. This I had learned from the adults. Even when I had an abscessed tooth and we couldn't afford a dentist, I still thought that my pain was just another occurrence and part of what happens during our lives. But sometimes good things also happened unexpectedly. One day, my father took me to see a circus in a big tent, which was erected by the British authority for the entertainment of the English community. He had been busy at work and didn't have time to express his enthusiasm, but I interpreted this as his deepest expression of love for me. Enthralled, I watched as men and women performed acrobatic acts and animals did tricks. That evening, I went to bed thinking about Saleh and Asad, and wondered how I would describe the bright costumes to them, or the beautiful women whose bare legs awakened in me an inexplicable curiosity, followed by a feeling of embarrassment.

As if to counterbalance the joy I had with my father, the next day my mother decided to offer her annual penance to God for the sins that she may have inadvertently committed and asked me to accompany her to Saint Elijah's church. I followed her on the narrow dirt path until we could see the shrine on the peak of Mount Carmel. Resting before our final climb, we stood still, looking at the many cement steps that separated us from the church. In preparation for our ascent, my mother took her sheer nylon stockings off and folded them carefully, making sure not to snag the delicate fabric with her fingernails. She knelt down on the first step and began to climb on her knees. I watched as they began to bleed. Without uttering a word, I walked by her side in a state of terror. The resolute expression on her face made me think that this act was a sacrament and a necessary rite that would help maintain our survival. I was utterly exhausted when we returned home and spent the early evening in my room, drifting in and out of sleep. I was awakened by my father's angry voice. "We have done enough penance for God!" he shouted. "Our daily hardships alone should be more than enough!"

The following morning, my mother seemed at peace with herself. She even looked satisfied when working in the kitchen. To our surprise, an Italian nun from the Sisters of the

Holy Family of Nazareth knocked on our door. My mother greeted her warmly and asked her in. The nun took out a rosary and gave it to my mother. Pleased to be in the company of someone who shared her religious beliefs, she spoke with enthusiasm. I listened to them talk about God and wondered if the nun might have been a reward for my mother's penance.

At the end of her visit, the nun talked about the dire need for food, and asked if we could spare some staples that other Palestinian families could have. Wanting to help, my mother momentarily forgot our own poverty and gave her the bag of lentils from the cupboard, most of the sugar in the glass jar, and half of the bread that she had baked earlier that day.

It was not until the nun had left our house that my mother suddenly looked apprehensive, glimpsing at the sugar jar that sat nearly empty on the kitchen countertop. I knew how hard my parents worked to conceal our poverty. My father was very creative. He often bought cheap furniture from the flea market in Haifa and restored it. My mother recycled fabric from garments purchased from the same market to make clothes for us and for others. Sometimes, I felt that the efforts made by my parents to mask our poverty were a much greater burden to them than all their other hardships combined. Seeing how happy she was, my father didn't complain when she told him about her gifts to the poor.

A month after my grandparents left Haifa, my parents took me to see them in Nazareth. To my surprise, they seemed quite settled. The lofts were stacked with new mattresses, and the dining room was furnished with a new dining set. It felt comfortable to be back in our original home, in a place where the neighbors spoke the same language. I was also surprised by the abundance of food in their house, and by my grandparents' ease with one another. They had established a comfortable indifference to what the other believed or had to say, and their sparse conversation seemed untinged by rancor.

My father was still cautious with his own father. Their conversation seemed to take effort, but it gradually led them to exchange information about their lives. It was on that evening that we learned my grandfather had set up a table and two chairs on the sidewalk near the British administrative offices in Nazareth. He was helping people with matters involving British law and other formalities that he was familiar with. With only paper and pen on his table, he made enough money for all their needs. He asked my father to consider moving back to the family home.

My mother and I were happy about the prospect of moving back to our home, but we weren't sure if my father would agree to it. After dinner, I went to see my friend Asad and told him about the possibility of our move back to Nazareth. He was happy, but not in the same way a child would be. He was more measured. He acted like an adult. His mother, who was in the same room, listening to our conversation, explained, "Asad is the man of the house now." This title was given to him after the death of his father. It was also a warning that things would not be the same between us if I returned.

My grandparents were eager to have us back. They spoke about the need for me to be at school with my friends. They also encouraged my father to quit his job in Haifa and told him to find work in Nazareth. He said that he preferred his full-time job with his English employer. Although I was extremely happy when we moved back to our home, I felt that something of me was left in Haifa, especially when I realized that my father would still be living on his own in the train car on the beach, and that I would only see him on his day off.

My grandfather began to speak openly about his time away from home. Attracted to his stories, neighbors often gathered on our veranda to hear him talk about his adventures. Confident and commanding respect, he looked like a different man. With the money he earned at his table, he bought more furniture for the house. A beautiful grandfather clock stood near the front hall and chimed on the hour. He made frequent trips to Haifa. He bought a writing desk and a beautiful compass from an English dealer. Our house began to look different from the others in the neighborhood. My grandfather's sudden interest in English instruments and furniture made my mother anxious. Despite her discomfort, he went to Haifa and bought a wind-up gramophone with English vinyl records. This attracted more people to our house. No one understood the music, but the pleasure was in seeing a machine sing. All this added to the mystery of the man who had suddenly reappeared. His spending habits began to arouse suspicion among people in the neighborhood. I feared that he might have been selling the gold wedding bands to the English dealers, and worried that his secret would be revealed.

Uncomfortable with our sudden wealth, some people began to treat us cautiously. In the past, we were the same as everyone else in the neighborhood. Time was never important to anyone, its passage each day was marked solely by sunrise and sunset, prayers from mosques, and church bells. Now the grandfather clock kept track of the day by seconds, minutes, and hours. Dalal complained that she could hear our clock from her house next door, and it was a constant reminder that life was ticking away. But my grandfather remained oblivious to what other people said. He continued to make visits to Haifa, where he bought a gold-plated pen that he placed in the top pocket of his suit.

It was my mother, the gentlest among us, who lost her temper first. She demanded that the clock and everything else be removed from the house. Taken aback, my grandfather tried to defend his actions, making a case for keeping up with the times, even though he knew that was not the issue at hand. She tried to tell him that his behavior had put us at odds with the neighbors, but he continued to argue his case. Everyone heard her screams when he refused to budge. It was not until she told him that he had lost his sanity that my grandmother and Dalal came out to rescue him, but also to convince him that my mother's demands were justified. After realizing that everyone was angry with him, he removed the weights off the chains, and the clock stopped ticking. He moved all his new acquisitions to the storage room. I was awestruck by my mother's hidden power. Even my grandmother was relieved. I heard her thank my mother when they were alone in the kitchen.

I felt bad for my grandfather, yet I understood how difficult it was for people in our neighborhood to understand a man who had been away for so long and had acquired customs and habits that were unknown to us. Fortunately, my mother's outburst made him more self-aware. He toned down his lifestyle.

Seeing my mother step out of her familiar character had been both thrilling and terrifying. I suspected that she was as surprised as the rest of us by her own burst of anger, but she soon returned to her usual self. There were no signs of gloating. I learned that the women around me handled victory with the same grace that they handled defeat. Still, it was evident that she had earned the respect of my grandfather, who, after this, never did anything without consulting her first. Living in close proximity to others, all events were shared, and nothing was concealed. Asad's mother, who had heard about my mother's outburst, decided to challenge what society had demanded of her son. She released him back into his childhood, and never called him the man of the house again. Instead, she claimed the title for herself.

My mother, who never had any interest in being anything other than a mother and a wife, was soon cast in the role of the strong and wise woman once others heard about the successful outcome of her rage. Other women came to seek her advice on all sorts of marital problems, wanting to learn how to stand up to a stubborn husband or a father-in-law. Not wanting to turn anyone away from her door, she listened and gave words of encouragement. These women left our house believing that they had been touched by her magical power. It only took a few weeks before the alliance between her and my grandmother began to deteriorate. Uncomfortable with my mother's elevated rank, my grandmother felt as if she had been robbed of her own wisdom earned by the passing of time. Their relationship became strained, and they kept their conversation limited to what was absolutely necessary.

I watched as my mother began to live up to her new role by actually giving advice and encouraging women to assert themselves. Gifts were given to her by the happy devotees, and suddenly our house was full of freshly pressed olive oil, white cheese, all kinds of fruit and vegetables, and even myrrh, which prompted my grandmother to sarcastically declare that she would not be surprised if my mother would soon be sainted. As usual, my father was too busy to notice what was going on, but my grandfather did, and he reveled in the fact that he and my mother were being rewarded for their brainpower, a skill that did not require physical toil.

Having more than we needed, she shared the gifts with the neighbors. Peace was regained when my mother began to solicit my grandmother's advice.

Much had changed in my life in that short period of time. The man who had lived formless in my imagination for most of my childhood was present in the flesh. I never stopped wondering about what he might do next.

Our house was the busiest on the street. People could be seen coming and going for most of the day. Tanous, the oud player in our neighborhood, looking for an audience, decided to bring his instrument with him on story night. Though my father was usually reserved, my mother encouraged him to accompany Dalal with a song while Tanous played the oud.

Dalal seemed, to me, to be just a younger friend of my grandmother. She was funny, daring, and told stories that I did not understand. She was also very vibrant and laughed more than the rest of us. Soon I began to notice how her hair rested on her shoulders when she was having her morning coffee in her nightgown. My eyes would drift to her body even when I wanted to look away. I often wondered what made Dalal so different from the rest of the women around her. I developed a slight fear of my own feelings when I was in her presence. I spent hours trying to decode her stories. One day I was walking with Asad and I decided to ask if he had any fears. He said that sometimes he feared that the sun would not return in the morning, and we would have to live in perpetual darkness. It was not the answer that I was looking for. I wanted to know if he was ever nervous around girls, but I didn't dare to ask him directly.

I felt shy around Dalal, and worried that everyone would see my interest in her. I stopped looking in her direction and always sat in the back when she told her stories. I did not understand why I felt as I did but couldn't talk about my feelings to anyone. I had always been drawn to her humor and funny anecdotes. I was never shy about using her language in the schoolyard. But this was different. It troubled me to no end. In time, however, I began to see that I was not the only one who was under her spell. A hush would fall on our veranda whenever she accompanied Tanous with a love song. All eyes would follow her every move. I began to understand that Dalal was a beautiful and voluptuous woman that everyone was attracted to.

With everyone keeping busy in our house, I was left alone to do whatever I wanted. Asad and I managed to smuggle the gramophone out of the storage room in a burlap sack. We took it to the abandoned Turkish post, just up the hill from our neighborhood, but far enough away that no one could hear us. We told the other kids on our street to follow us, and we spent the entire day taking turns cranking and listening to English music. We did the same thing every day, taking the gramophone in and out of my house without detection. One day, two mounted British police officers, drawn to the English music, burst into our hiding place and found us dancing. We were marched out of there and through the streets of Nazareth, followed by the gramophone, mounted on a horse. Accused of possessing stolen property, we were detained at the police station.

It didn't take long for our parents to be alerted. My grandfather assured the officer in charge that he had bought the gramophone in Haifa, but the officer demanded proof of ownership. He went home and returned with the receipt. My friends and I, along with the gramophone, were released. In a fit of anger and defiance, my grandfather smashed the gramophone on the ground of the police station. We followed him out with our heads down. He was so upset by the officer's accusations that he left me alone and I was never punished. After a short time, the incident was forgotten, but, even at the age of twelve, I felt changed by the experience. I realized that I was living under the scrutiny of a much higher power, greater than that of my parents.

After another school year came to an end, we didn't go to the train car on the beach as we had done in the previous year. My grandfather advised against it, as resistance to British rule in Palestine began to intensify, and he felt that it would not be safe for us, or even for my father to be there on his own at night. My father also began to complain about his employer's sudden change of attitude toward him, which he did not understand, as he was still a devoted worker. Threatened by the militant opposition to the British rule, the Englishman vented his anger by blaming my father for allowing my grandmother to teach Edmund Arabic. He said that even after months of being away from my grandmother, his wife still had to put bitters on his son's tongue every time he spoke it, yet, she couldn't make him stop. I felt sorry for Edmund when my father recounted the story to us. Upset by his mother's cruelty, my grandmother used harsh language for the first time. She cursed Edmund's mothers for tormenting an innocent child.

I felt more responsible when Saleh asked me to help him with the early morning bread delivery to the disabled men and women in our town. They were mostly elderly and depended on society to care for them. They lived in small rooms given to them by merchants who lived near the market. Saleh's mother made sure that the first batch out of the oven was put aside for them. On one of our deliveries, I recognized a dress that I had seen my mother make worn by a woman who gave us a shy smile and muttered blessings for our hands. It was also during our deliveries that I met a man named Hadi, who drew beautiful pictures on the white walls of his small room. With only pieces of charcoal, he was able to produce drawings of people and animals with amazing accuracy.

I loved being with my friends in the early morning, but we soon realized that it was not going to be the carefree summer we were accustomed to, as the British military presence increased around us. The atmosphere in our house also changed, when men who lived in the neighborhood began to meet on our veranda. Wanting to protect the frail men and women who lived among them from the clashes between the rebels and the British forces that took place at night, the merchants in the market asked my father to install latches on their doors.

Dalal was chosen for her cheerful personality to accompany him and soothe the worries of the men and women who had lived with open doors all their lives. While most people would feel vulnerable without a lock on their door at night, the lock signaled danger to the disabled men and women and made them feel isolated.

One week later, the woman whose dress I'd recognized as one that my mother had sewn died. Everyone speculated that she had died from fright. She was a stranger who had wandered into our town, and her religious background was unknown, so she received her religious rights at the cemetery from an Imam and a priest. Fearing additional deaths, my father removed the latches. A group of men were selected to patrol the streets. Gunfire could be heard at night, and I remember walking to Saleh's store in the morning through a street littered with shiny bullet casings. Our parents, fearful for our safety, began to curtail our activities and kept watchful eyes on us. My friends and I could not leave our neighborhood and had to report our whereabouts often. Story night, however, continued once a week. Dalal, who gave the impression that everything was fine, was the bright light in our lives. Unfazed by the menacing events, she sang and lifted our spirits.

Delivering bread to the disabled men and women was the only thing that Saleh and I continued to do. We put on our bravest face and acted as though everything was normal when we went to see Hadi, who always seemed more nervous than the others. I saved the coal that burnt in the brazier on story nights for him, and I could see him trying to find a space for a new drawing on his walls.

The increased violence also made my grandfather nervous, and he stopped going to work. He sat behind his desk at home for most of the day writing and drawing streetscapes. On the second day, I realized that he was working on a defense plan. Everyone was happy to have him in charge. They felt he was the natural choice for a leader. We soon began work building barricades to block access to vehicles through the already narrow streets in our old neighborhood. Dalal was selected by my grandfather to keep an eye on the women and children whose fathers had joined the rebels, and to make sure that their needs for food were met. His choice was received with the approval of everyone. Not one dissenting voice was heard, even when Dalal began to sit with the men on story night. To stop the rebels, the British district commissioner, Lewis Yelland Andrews, introduced harsh measures, and heavier gunfire attacks against the rebels were heard at night.

We returned to our everyday lives, but I began to notice that, despite my grandfather's apparent composure, he never left the house without me by his side. I knew that he was feeling vulnerable when he began to show interest in what I was doing. He even thanked me for being his companion when he first returned from Turkey. My grandfather's vulnerability gave me strength, and I worried less at night. I also began to see more clearly that the power in our house was constantly shifting hands. It felt as though I was next in line when my grandfather began to repeatedly ask me to stay by his side. Even Dalal seemed to want me by her side. She began to ask me to accompany her when she went to the market. I naively believed that no harm could come to me when I was in her presence. I didn't know that battles were also raging between the rebels and the British troops in the rest of the country, and that they could, at any moment, escalate into a full war that would engulf Nazareth. I should have known that something was amiss when my mother began to embrace my father before he left for work, and when my grandmother spent more time than usual in prayer.

On his own initiative, Asad decided that we should reenforce the barricades. We spent many days rolling rocks from the hills around our neighborhood to our street and buttressing the existing barriers that the adults built. Water in clay jugs was left outside on the steps of homes for us to drink. But work still felt like play. We enjoyed the attention, and no one seemed to object to what we were doing. Even my grandfather came to inspect our work, and he suggested that we should continue to narrow the openings to make it more difficult for mounted soldiers to get through. Asad listened carefully to my grandfather's instructions. My grandfather's visit ended what we had thought of as play. Inspired by my grandfather's authority, Asad changed his attitude and became more demanding of us.

In September of 1937, the rebels killed Lewis Yelland Andrews, the British commissioner, near Christ Church in Nazareth, not far from where we lived. Fearing retribution, our school closed its doors. My grandfather retreated to his bed or the veranda with Hadi by his side, worried about severe retaliation and his own safety. Terrified by the shelling, Hadi had to be moved to our house. Both men sat and listened to the sound of gunfire going off in the distance. My grandfather's fear originated from the atrocities he had witnessed, and his knowledge of what humans were capable of doing to one another.

My father stayed in Haifa upon his employer's insistence once travel became difficult. He slept in the train car on the beach, causing my grandfather and the rest of us to fear for his safety. When Asad and I were scared, we walked to the barriers that we helped build and shifted and adjusted the stones, making sure that the street was narrow enough to prevent British military vehicles from going through. It was an activity that made us feel safe. One night, when the shelling was particularly heavy, I prayed to Saint Elijah and asked him to protect my father, who was within his sight on the beach. As the struggle throughout the country intensified, and our own existence hung in the balance, another quiet rebellion began to take place within our family's ranks, when Dalal and my grandmother took on responsibilities usually reserved for men. They organized food drives to aid families who had lost men to imprisonment or death.

Wanting to return some semblance of order to our lives, and hoping that the assassination of the British commissioner was a victory that would keep the British out of Nazareth, Dalal and my grandmother decided to remove the barriers from our street. Asad and I, along with the other neighborhood boys, were entrusted with the task of returning the rocks that we had brought down from the hills. Eager to please, Asad worked hard. He didn't stop until a large boulder rolled back and crushed his right arm. He was taken to the English hospital, and the arm was amputated.

Asad's mother, unable to cope, decided to take him and his sisters back to her parents' house in a village near the Lebanese border. Being directly across the narrow street that separated our houses, Asad's home became a dark void at night. The oil lamp that used to flicker in his room, and which he had used to send me signals, was forever gone. I never saw Asad again. Many of my friends, including Saleh, began to leave Nazareth. They went to live on farms with relatives in smaller towns. Without my friends, I stopped going out to play. Hadi, seeing how lonely I felt without my friends, drew a life-size image of Asad on my bedroom wall with his arm restored, holding the football that we had fashioned from our old clothes.

Noticing that it was no longer used, my grandmother unraveled the football, washed it, and hung the cloth strips on the line to dry. With so many of my friends gone, I began to spend more time with Hadi. On days when the shelling was light and the sun was shining, I sat on the veranda with my grandfather and Hadi, who was still living with us. Dalal, who had been the soul of our neighborhood, now looked anxious, and her singing stopped once people stopped gathering on our veranda.

My family moved around the house without saying much to each other. As if to remind everyone that my father was still in Haifa, we began to talk about him whenever we sat to eat our dinner. My grandfather took the hint and vowed to bring him home. A few days later, he used what little strength he had and traveled to Haifa. He returned a day later with my father by his side.

That night, my mother and grandmother made a sumptuous meal. Dalal sang. I was so happy that I danced for the first time. My happiness, however, didn't last long. It was marred when a British policeman bludgeoned Tanous, the musician, for marching in a political rally. I watched Dalal use the cleaned strips of what used to be my football to wind around his bloodied head.

YILDIZ THE TURKISH WOMAN

Yildiz was known in our neighborhood as the Turkish widow, even though everyone knew that her husband was still alive. She had been only a young bride when Britain defeated the Ottomans, and her husband marched along with the rest of the Turkish soldiers out of Palestine. However, like many other Turkish individuals who had not known another country, she stayed stubbornly in her matrimonial home on our street, despite the hostility some people still felt toward the Turkish people.

On my way to school, I walked by her house. I grew accustomed to seeing her sitting on the stone step of her front door with a worried expression on her face. But one day, I saw her sitting on the very edge of her doorstep in the rain. Her face was alight with childish pleasure, and she stared at the handmade colorful paper boats that the neighborhood children were launching from a higher elevation into the open gutter, which served as a runoff for storm water. Noticing how enthralled she looked, I intercepted a red one and gave it to her. In return, she smiled at me and took it inside her house. Seeing how pleased she was, I decided to make one for her to enjoy the next time it rained. After folding the paper into the shape of a boat, I decorated it with small banners, and waited for the rain to come.

Not long after, while walking back from school, I saw a British policeman with his interpreter, trying to take Yildiz away against her will. Frightened, I ran home and alerted my mother about what was happening. It took only a few minutes for all the women who lived close by to circle the men and demand an explanation. Through his interpreter, the policeman said that he meant no harm and was only there on behalf of the British authority, who wanted to repatriate Turkish nationals back to their homeland. But Yildiz said that Palestine was the only home she had ever known, and that her parents were born and buried in Jerusalem, the city of her own birth. Not wanting a confrontation with the women, the policeman decided to leave, and a very grateful Yildiz thanked the women for their help and thanked me for saving her. On that same day, my mother stopped calling her "the Turkish woman" and began to use her name. She even paid her a visit after the incident. Yildiz, however, was nervous around my mother and the rest of the women in the neighborhood. She appeared to feel at ease only with the children who lived nearby. I never knew what it meant to be a branch cut off from a tree until my grandmother described Yildiz in this way.

Soon after, I was walking back from school when Yildiz invited me in. She handed me a box of date cookies in gratitude for coming to her aid. Once I stepped inside, I saw immediately that her house was different from others in the neighborhood. The air was scented with delicate perfumes, and her furniture was of a much finer quality. She also had an oud, a string instrument, on the edge of her soft daybed. It was more beautiful than any other oud that I had seen. The wooden inlay was rare and exotic. Its face was embedded with stars made of mother-of-pearl. I assumed that it must have belonged to her husband, but seeing how enthralled I was with it, she picked it up and began to play. She even sang for me. Her eyes lit up and her body began to sway to the rhythm of her music. For the rest of the week, I thought of nothing else, and I longed to see her again.

I was allowed to re-enter her house when, with my father's permission, she began to teach me how to play the oud. She said that I had a special gift for music. She always made me wash my hands in a basin filled with rose-scented water. She even combed my hair before I sat down for my lesson. She was not like the other women in our neighborhood, who had already given birth to several children and were busy caring for them. A childless woman, she was thin and graceful. Her body moved with such ease that she could be mistaken for a child. She was only a little taller than me when we stood side by side, and this made it easier for me to imagine that she was close to my own age, even though I knew many years separated us. I loved being in her house and listened carefully to her stories, especially the one describing her childhood home in Jerusalem, where she could see the Dome of the Rock from her bedroom window.

One day, Yildiz said that she was going to invite some families who lived in the vicinity to come hear me play. In preparation for the event, I spent several evenings practicing in her living room. I stopped taking interest in what my friends were doing and began to behave like the older boys at my school. Curiosity about the Turkish woman who could play the oud was probably the real reason why people came to hear me play. My mother and father sat on the main divan, along with my grandmother. Chairs were placed in a row for others. After welcoming the neighbors with cups of coffee, she sat me on a chair, and I began to play. Everyone stopped talking, and I could see my father's chest swelling with pride. My mother sat smiling, but my grandmother looked sullen. Cheers erupted when I stopped, and I was asked to play again.

On the way home, everyone was pleased and complimented me on my talent, except for my grandmother. She felt that my skills were achieved by sorcery. She even washed my hands with holy water given to her by our priest on Palm Sunday. I was upset with her for thinking that Yildiz was a sorceress, but I was also pleased to see that my parents didn't share her views and were very proud of me. Later that evening, while we were sitting around the dining table, my mother said that Abla, our neighbor, was thinking of asking Yildiz to teach her son to play the oud. Hearing that, my grandmother's face stiffened, and she said, "Abla's child does not know the difference between his foot and hand." She was not a mean woman. This was her way of saying that I was special, as well as her apology to me for thinking that my talent was achieved through sorcery.

Several months had gone by since the musical gathering, but I still hadn't done anything special for Yildiz. The rain had not come, and I still had the paper boat that I wanted to float by her house sitting on my table. I also wanted to buy her something from the market, but I didn't have any money. Christmas was still months away, too long for me to wait for the few shillings that I always received from my uncle Boutros and the one shilling I got from my father after kissing his hand. I knew my friend Kamal was always able to extract money from English soldiers who came to visit the Church of the Annunciation, so I decided to accompany him in hopes of learning how to get money from the foreign visitors. It was not hard. All Kamal had to do was feign his delight at seeing the English soldiers and to welcome them to Palestine. My father had always been a proponent of independence for Palestine, so I knew this was wrong, but it was the only way I could accomplish my mission. I would have done anything for Yildiz, and this simple act didn't seem that horrible, so I copied Kamal and stood by the church door to welcome the soldiers to Palestine.

In an hour, I made so much money that I could hear it jingle in my pocket as I ran home. I spent an entire week looking at shop windows and trying to figure out what to buy Yildiz. I knew that whatever I bought would have to fit in my schoolbag, as I didn't want anyone to see me carrying a gift to her house. In the end, I decided to buy something that we could share. I bought a small box of baklava. I ran to Yildiz, placing my hand over my bag, trying to conceal the shape of the box that protruded through the worn-out cloth of my school satchel. Bursting with pride, I took the box out and gave it to her. She was so happy that she kissed me on the cheek, then asked if I loved her. Blushing, I was unable to speak and only shook my head up and down.

That day, she played the oud and sang a Turkish song, I could not understand, but the melody sounded very sad, and tears rolled down her cheeks. Frightened by her sadness, I excused myself and left. She never cried in my presence again, but I knew that she was truly sad. Since she was alone and didn't have any children to raise, she spent most of her time reading or playing her oud. Unlike the other women in the neighborhood, she spoke three languages: Turkish, French, and Arabic. She was fluent in Arabic but had a Turkish accent. My grandmother diagnosed this as an inflection without a cure, for she believed that a mother tongue could only be obtained through mother's milk. I felt angry with my grandmother for saying such things about her. So, I began to correct her pronunciation. It amused her at first, but after a while she began to curb and restrain her speech, and the ease that she felt when we were together disappeared.

The sudden change between us made me sad, and I wished that others could see how nice she was and love her as I did. I didn't understand why the women in our neighborhood prevented the British police from taking her away by protecting her, yet left her alone after the incident.

I felt older when the rain finally arrived in late fall, and therefore decided not to float the little paper boat that I had made for Yildiz. I began to spend more time with my friend Kamal, sitting on the steps that led to the Church of the Annunciation next to our school, but I didn't want to participate when Kamal welcomed the British soldiers. I even refused their shillings when they tried to put them in my hand. Kamal stopped talking to me when one day, I tossed a cap belonging to an English soldier on the ground after he tried to put it on my head for the amusement of his friends. Fearful of the soldier's reaction, I ran away and hid in the mosque that was just around the corner.

My father was summoned to school after Kamal reported the incident to the priest, and I received a warning of my dismissal from school. My father listened politely, but when the priest continued to scold me, he lost his temper, and we left the meeting. On the way home, I walked by his side without saying a word. I felt that he was not angry with me. Fearing that I was going to get the strap, I didn't go to school the next day. I pretended that I was sick and stayed in my bed for the whole day. I knew that I couldn't hide in my bed forever, so I returned the following day. Kamal, who usually sat in the back row, had been moved to the front as a reward for his good behavior toward the British soldiers. I was moved from the middle row to the back.

Walking home at the end of my school day, I noticed that Yildiz's front window was smashed. She sat on the doorstep and stared at the shattered glass. I sat next to her for a while, but I was not sure if she wanted me by her side, so I went home to get my father. Being a carpenter, he quickly replaced the glass and made shutters for her window, but she still seemed deeply scared. She said that someone had broken her window in the middle of the night. She had crawled under her bed and didn't come out until the morning, and this was where she continued to sleep for the next few days.

It was difficult for me to understand how frightened she was, especially at a time when our house was bustling with festivities in celebration of my uncle Boutros's wedding. Relatives came to our house every evening for the *taalil*, a pre-wedding party that typically lasts for a whole month and continues until the wedding day. With so many of my cousins at our house, I stopped going out, but continued to think about Yildiz. Still too innocent to understand race relations, I wondered why anyone would break her window, and questioned my own parents' decision not to invite her to my uncle's wedding. She was a close neighbor and could have provided music with her oud, instead of Musa Ibrahim.

Musa Ibrahim was a blind Jewish musician who lived in Tiberia. He was accompanied by his young son, who carried his oud and guided his steps. Musa was favored over all other musicians in Galilee and was hired only by those who could afford his fees. He was treated with the utmost respect, and it was said that his musical talent was obtained through a barter with the Creator, who took his sight in exchange. On the night before my uncle's wedding, Hagop, the Armenian photographer, arrived to photograph the traditional groom shaving party. The expression on his pleasant face was marred by a contemptuous look, which he extended to all who shared physical similarities with Ottoman Turks. By contrast, Khasan, his Circassian assistant, whose family had also sought refuge in Palestine after the Russian conquest of the Caucasus, endeared himself to us by smiling at all times.

The old tradition of giving the groom the best shave of his life was the last rite and the culmination of a month-long celebration. This was an emotional time for my uncle and his friends. He was about to forsake all his friends for his bride who lived in Haifa. Ahmed the barber arrived and began to lather the shaving soap on my uncle's face, while Musa Ibrahim played the oud and sang. My uncle's ecstatic friends danced, while the women in our family echoed Musa's Ibrahim praise for the bride and groom. Even my overjoyed grandmother sprang to her feet and danced. Her steps were so light, she could have been dancing on a cloud.

It was near midnight when all of a sudden, the British police arrived at our house and took my uncle away. He had been seen the previous week hurling stones at the mounted policemen who were attempting to disperse an anti-British rally. His photo was captured by an English journalist. The joyful songs from minutes before turned into wails, and ended what would have been one of the happiest days of my grandmother's life. Everyone at the celebration was sent home.

My life was not the same after my grandmother took to her bed. Fearing that she was going to die, I refused to go to school and remained by her side. I only went out once, when my mother sent me to buy food from the market. There, I saw Yildiz. She seemed hurt when I went to greet her and asked why I had stopped coming for oud lessons. I told her that I was busy taking care of my sick grandmother and promised to resume the lessons once she felt better. Looking at her as she walked away, I realized that she was no longer the young girl that I had once imagined her to be. Reluctant steps had replaced her agile gait. Her basket seemed enormous next to her delicate body. I continued to watch until she disappeared around the bend, then felt an inexplicable sadness.

School stopped being important when clashes worsened between the British forces and the Palestinian rebels. My grandmother stayed in her bed even when her friends came to visit. Laments replaced their lively conversations. They stopped coming when my grandmother's health deteriorated and she was no longer responsive to her surroundings. Our entire neighborhood became dull. People stopped caring for their gardens, since the activity seemed meaningless. I was not under any pressure to return to school, especially when my father, who was hard of hearing, was recruited by the rebels to man the lookout on the hills around Nazareth. He stood up all night long with a gun in his hand, straining his ears, staring nervously in all directions, ready to report approaching English soldiers to the men who were camped in the wooded area below his lookout.

My grandmother's condition worsened when she found out that the rebels had recruited my father. She stopped eating and died a few weeks later. There had been so many fatalities by then that the death of an old woman didn't seem to stir any sadness in our neighborhood. Everyone continued with their lives as if nothing had happened at all. But I was heartbroken by her death, and my sadness was so overwhelming that I never went back to school. Fearful of the clashes on the street, and of what might happen to me if I left the house, I stayed with my mother and my sisters.

My father was fighting a war not of his own choosing. His absence caused tremendous worry for my mother. I heard her tell a neighbor that she tried to point out the strategic flaw of having a nearly deaf man on the lookout in Nazareth. She begged for my father's release. But the rebel leader felt that a nervous person was the ideal choice for a night watchman and dismissed my mother's concerns. Attempting to soothe my fears, my mother reported that my father was a brave hero who was going to keep us safe, but then she broke out into tears.

Seeing how my mother was struggling to keep us fed, I put my pride aside and asked my friend Kamal if I could accompany him to the church steps in hopes of making some money. That day, I sat on the steps long after Kamal had left and grinned at tourists and soldiers who came to visit the church, welcoming them to Palestine. I soon earned enough money to buy a bag of lentils for my mother and an almond nougat for myself. Walking home, I noticed Yildiz peering at me through the shutters that my father had made for her. She didn't open her window or come out to greet me as she used to do.

Terror began to dominate my life when the adults around me could no longer hide their fear. I had never seen my parents exhibit religious feelings at home, and first felt reassured when my mother began to recite a morning prayer of gratitude. But her prayers then turned into a scolding monologue with God. I interpreted her angry and haphazard prayers as no more than a superstitious attempt to appease a God she no longer believed in. I watched in dismay as she began to slip into despair, just as my grandmother had.

The increased presence of British troops in Nazareth caused the rebels to move to an undisclosed location. In compensation for my father's total absence, my mother began to receive a large sack of bread flour at the end of each month. On days when she was aggravated, my mother vented her anger by punching the cloth flour sack. We watched as the loosened flour made a cloud of dust. Yet she was always happy when a new one was delivered to our house at the end of the month. My sisters and I spent the day in our grandmother's room playing with objects that we were forbidden to touch when she was alive. My sisters could even play with the gold jewelry that my grandmother had treasured.

Perhaps out of habit, our mother acted as if our grandmother was still alive. She didn't seem to worry about us when we were in her room. Unlike my younger sisters, who could be distracted with gold, I felt lonely and spent much of my day lying on my grandmother's bed, lost in a perpetual state of fear, and losing track of how much time had passed since my father had been gone. This feeling deepened when the large flour sack that marked the end of the month stopped coming. All efforts seemed meaningless. Without our allowance of bread flour, I spent more time on the church steps begging for coins so I could buy food for my family.

I only became aware of the passing of time when I realized that my sisters had become older. My own age, however, was revealed in a cruel way, when the tourists and soldiers stopped giving me money as I welcomed them to Palestine. My voice deepened, and I was no longer able to invoke sympathy from the English visitors. I was no longer a charming little boy.

Seeing how unhappy I was, my mother suggested that I resume my oud lessons. I agreed, hoping that the pleasant atmosphere and the nice fragrance in Yildiz's house would cheer me up. But everything in it had changed since my last visit. The sweet rose water scent in her living room had changed to a musty odor, and her shiny hair had turned dull. Comforted by my presence, she tried to smile, but her parted lips only conveyed her despair. I moved close to her and held her hand as I had seen my father do when he wanted to console my mother, but she let go and moved away to the farthest corner in the room. Not knowing what to do, I apologized, then left her house. Dejected, I walked to church and sat on the steps with my hand stretched out, but I was chased away by the priest.

Feeling vengeful, I went home and stole my grandmother's gold cross. I sold it to a jeweler whom I had seen melt down old jewelry in a hot cauldron. I bought food for my mother. That night, and many nights to follow, my grandmother appeared in my dreams warning me that worse times were yet to come. I spent the rest of my youth watching our country go through terrible hardship under British rule. I tried to imagine what could possibly be worse than the lives we were already living, while bracing myself for what might come next.

Under the Gaze of Angels

I was born in Haifa, during the British Mandate for Palestine, on August 21, 1945. My British birth certificate and baptismal document states a name that is different from the one I use today. My parents named me Maurice for reasons I can only speculate. They never explained their choice. Today, I suspect that it was done to appease the new British rulers, who unseated the Ottomans who ruled Palestine. They hoped that my name would make my life easier when dealing with them. I lived with that name for the first few years of my life.

According to my mother, I was reluctant to embrace life and struggled with every breath. My acute asthma required constant care and, lacking funds, my parents abandoned the treatments offered by modern medicine, deciding to explore the traditional remedies practiced in our community. Their search took them to a sage, who sensed, upon seeing me, that something was terribly wrong. Hearing my name, he cursed the devil. To rid me of bad blood, he took his sharp knife and bled me by making small incisions all over my back, then proceeded with a name-changing ceremony and gave me my Arabic name. He called me Said, restoring me to what he viewed to be a normal state.

My new name, however, didn't cure my asthma. In fact, my condition worsened when my family was driven out of Haifa by the increased violence between the local inhabitants and the Jewish groups who began to come from Europe in greater numbers, wanting to claim Palestine as their own. We left behind our home and my father's bombed-out carpentry workshop. Abandoning all of their large possessions for the sake of our safety, my parents collected whatever they could carry and fled to Nazareth. There, we took shelter in the basement of the Sisters of Nazareth Convent and waited for the conflict to end. Many vacant homes had been left in trust to various religious institutions by the frightened people who had decided to escape the violence in Palestine. They moved to neighboring Arab countries, thinking that they could reclaim their homes when the conflict was sorted out. With the establishment of Israel in 1948, the borders were permanently sealed. Realizing that no one was coming back to their homes, the religious institutions made a decision. They allowed people living in their corridors and basements to move into the vacant homes that had been left in their care. In a dramatic twist of fate, we ended up in one of the most beautiful vacant houses in Nazareth.

Nazareth

The move to our new home was upsetting for me at first, but I soon began to feel comfortable. The angels painted on the living room ceiling kept a constant watch and made me feel safe. The large window framed a perfect view of the Church of the Annunciation, the white mosque, and our new place of worship—the Melkite Greek Catholic church, with Byzantine rites going back to the early Christians of Antioch.

Not fully aware of the catastrophe that had befallen my family, I ventured throughout the house, exploring its many distinct and lavish details. Spanning the entire front, the long balcony made it possible for me to have a bird's-eye view of the garden below. With my two older sisters, Najla and Layla, in school, and my brother Souheil still in his crib, I had the run of the house, and the full attention of my mother. The clock tower in the monastery, which stood next to the Church of the Annunciation, was directly across from our balcony. It was close enough that, if my mother squinted, she could tell the time. When it was hot outside, I would move into the living room and lie down on the cool marble floor. Captivated by the angels on the ceiling and the calligraphy on the banners below, I assumed that they held a mystery that I would solve once I had learned how to read. I often closed my eyes and fell asleep, overwhelmed by the immense complexity of our ceiling.

Entrusted with the duty of lookout for my aunt Miriam's arrival, I stood on the balcony and tried to remember her. It had been a long time since I last saw her. In Nazareth, I had four aunts and two uncles: all maternal relatives. Their faces were so familiar that I knew every dimple and expression. However, Aunt Miriam was my father's sister. She lived with the rest of his family in the village of Shefa-'Amr, just a short distance away. But, with the travel restriction imposed on Palestinians by the new Israeli government, we were unable to see them.

Aunt Miriam and her two sons had been granted an emergency travel permit because she needed surgery to repair a broken hip and leg. Her release from the English hospital in Nazareth was conditional. She was advised to stay close by in case she needed further treatment. Seated on a chair and carried by her sons, she appeared on the open staircase leading to our house. I ran back into the living room to alert my mother, but she didn't bother to look. Instead, she rushed around putting final touches on the quilted mat and cushions, where my aunt was eventually put down. My mother welcomed her and asked how she was, not in a direct manner, but in the customary way required in such a grave situation. "May your release from the hospital signal a blessing," she said, before serving the lemonade she had prepared.

My aunt took a sip and put the glass down. "The English doctor said that I may never walk again." Without waiting for my mother to express her sympathy, she looked at me and asked, "Little one, tell me, will I ever walk again?"

Frightened by the force of her question, I quickly answered, "Yes." The moment I uttered the word, the church bell rang. Believing it to be a good omen, my aunt rejoiced and asked me to sit by her side. With so many churches and bells ringing at different intervals, it was not unusual to have words punctuated by a bell. But this was the land of prophets, where even a prophecy by a small child had the power to annul the English doctor's diagnosis. My prediction paved the way for a special and long-lasting relationship with my aunt.

My mother was happy to have Aunt Miriam with us. She had many stories to tell, and since she couldn't move around, she didn't interfere in the kitchen. She accepted her food and the help we gave her with great courtesy. The only thing that bothered my mother was having to abandon a certain evening ritual. Ordinarily, she would place her chair on the balcony facing the mosque and wait for the muezzin to reach the top of the minaret to recite his prayers. Fearing that my aunt would judge her as greedy for requiring two faiths to save her soul, she abandoned the ritual. Being a Christian woman did not prevent my mother from embracing some aspects of Islam.

My mother feared disease and protected us with daily prayers and a good wash. During the day, she would shower us with praise and tell us how beautiful we were, but at night she would become stern and say that she had useless children. She was a sane and intelligent woman, but it was a common belief among many people in the region that, by understating the value of children, you make them less desirable to the evil spirits. Losing her first male child to a mysterious illness made my mother anxious. She followed the ritual vehemently.

I liked having my aunt in our house. Her stories were not the traditional tales describing the glorious past of incredibly rich and powerful Sultans, but consisted of factual retellings of her daily encounters with ordinary people and even the animals on her farm. Without malice, she talked about the frisky young horse that refused to have her on his back and threw her to the ground. She said that the horse was a free spirit, and no matter how hard she tried, he refused to accept her as master. In time, I was able to see that she was eager to return to her family. She began to supplement my prophecy with prayers, asking God for a speedy recovery. Her vivid stories helped me form an image of her farm, and I looked forward to the day when I could visit her there.

I was ten years old when my father took me to Shefa-'Amr, my paternal grandfather's home and my father's birthplace. Although I was staying with Aunt Miriam, tradition required us to start our visit at my grandparents' house. Climbing the steep staircase, we arrived at an open veranda, where a small windmill was attached to a wall, studded with little flags. The windmill spun eagerly, exhaling the air through its blades and causing the flags to flutter, producing an eerie sense of urgency in a house that was otherwise quiet.

Hearing a knock on the door must have been a moment of deep joy for my grandmother, but her face struggled to express happiness. She acted as if we were frequent visitors. My father bowed his head, attempting to kiss his mother's hand, but, being modest, she pulled it away, saying that she did not deserve such an honor. Fearing that she would try to refuse my kiss, I took her hand quickly and kissed it. In exchange, I received many blessings. I stood there gazing at her stooped body and wrinkled, pleasant face. Even at my young age, I was able to sense her sorrowful resignation. She was unsure of her words and spoke reluctantly. Unlike my relationship with my maternal grandmother in Nazareth, whom I had grown to love through daily interaction, my paternal grandmother was almost a stranger. I stood there trying to remember how many times I had seen her face. I knew it had only been a few, but I still felt a deep love for her.

Greeting my grandfather was an entirely different experience. He was far from shy and retiring. He received us with a hand raised and ready to be kissed. He spoke to my father in a tone that seemed formal for a conversation between a father and son. I was ignored. As if inconvenienced by our visit, he asked us to sit, and immediately asked my grandmother to make a pot of coffee. I was surprised when her stooped body sprang into action. She returned to the room moments later, balancing a tray with two cups of coffee, and a glass of water for me.

As my father and grandfather discussed the political changes in Palestine, I kept myself busy by counting the books in his bookcase. Although the bookcase was of a moderate size, he referred to it as his library. His room also contained a large writing desk. A shelf lined with medicine bottles which he distilled from plants cultivated on his own land hung above the desk. My grandfather had been a schoolteacher in his youth, but also an herbalist. It was the latter to which he had devoted his life after retirement. He also reported the weather to the farmers in his village and the hired help on his land. His mornings were spent caring for the health of farmers in the surrounding area. His afternoons were spent reading and receiving friends.

The room also contained some of his handwritten poems in frames. A framed letter from an English professor endorsing his medicinal cures was featured prominently on his desk. Drawn to the glass medicine bottles, I fingered the flasks, but sensing his unease, I promptly moved away and went to look at the framed photographs of my aunts and uncles, and a photo of my father as a young man standing next to his sister, Miriam. I was reminded of the real reason for our visit to Shefa-'Amr. I had not seen my aunt for a few years and grew anxious for us to be on our way.

Aunt Miriam's husband greeted us when we arrived. He was seated outside, looking rather gloomy and contemplative.

The wrinkles on his sad face indicated that his unhappiness had been long in the making. I searched his face for traces of joy, but none were visible. Since he sported a large mustache, his mouth was completely covered, making his expression undetectable. When my aunt appeared, I noticed how her body dipped to one side as she walked. She rushed toward me with open arms, her face beaming. "You were right, my little prophet. See, I can walk!"

I was thrilled to see that her spirit was still intact. Not even her limp could detract from her dignity. Her face shone with intelligence, and her two braids framed deep-set brown eyes and a delicate nose. Back then, I would have said that she was in her early forties, but she already had five children, all of whom were older than me, except for Najat, who was already an efficient helper on the farm.

After dinner, my father went back to Nazareth. I was left to spend the summer with my aunt and her family. She knew that I was eager to see the stables and took me for a tour. The animals, unaccustomed to seeing her at that time of the day, were excited, and answered her greeting. I also learned that evening that the greater part of her land was outside of the village and scattered in different locations.

I spent my first week getting to know my relatives and the children in her neighborhood. My aunt taught me how to do some chores, such as collecting eggs and feeding the animals. I took great delight in these new experiences. I also enjoyed the freedom that she granted me. Unlike my mother, she was fearless, and trusted me with tasks that my mother considered dangerous. As time went by, I began to feel secure among my relatives and the many neighbors who gathered in her courtyard in the evening for coffee and conversation. My cousin Najat and I were always included in these gatherings, but on one particular night, my aunt reminded us that we had to be up at four o'clock in the morning and sent us to bed.

Not used to waking up so early, I struggled to open my eyes. With my cousin's urging, I put my clothes on and walked out to the front yard, where three saddled horses stood in the dark. Having never sat on an animal before, I was reluctant to approach, but my aunt assured me that I would be safe. With my cousin's help, I mounted the horse, and we followed my aunt, who led the way to her farm. We rode through a wooded area followed by my aunt's dog, a large German Shepherd. Riding on a big horse was exhilarating. For the first time in my life, I felt strong and capable. The faint light on the horizon signaled the imminent approach of dawn and revealed the silhouettes of old olive groves.

After nearly two hours in the saddle, Aunt Miriam called out that we had arrived. My cousin and I spent the morning helping her with small tasks in a huge watermelon field, then went for a swim in a small pond on her farm. That evening, my aunt took us to the wedding of a Bedouin girl. Her nomadic family had pitched their tents on her land. In exchange, they helped my aunt by tending to and guarding the crops.

After greeting the family, we were ushered into a large tent. Fascinated by the event, I sat still and listened as the silver coins that were attached to the bride's headscarf jingled every time she moved her head. Even though they had tried to use makeup so she would look older, I could still see that she was almost a child. Her clanswomen stood outside, praising her in chants, while the women on the groom's side ululated in acknowledgment at the end of each song. The groom arrived, dismounted, and walked into the tent, where his bride was timidly waiting. He gathered her up in his arms and carried her back to his horse. She sat behind him and they bolted off, followed by his cheering tribesmen.

At the end of the evening, we rode our horses back to the storage shed, where my aunt kept a large straw mat. After we cleared a small area of rocks and pebbles, we placed the mat on the ground and spread three narrow quilted mats on top of it. The bed was comfortable, but I could not sleep. Unaccustomed to sleeping outside, I feared that a snake might crawl into my bed. To soothe my worries, my aunt asked me to collect pebbles. We placed them in a circle around the mats, while chanting a prayer that I repeated until she declared the area free of snakes. We returned to bed, and I promptly fell asleep.

The next morning, we rode a short distance away to look in on another Bedouin family. A young woman greeted us. She was seated on a makeshift bench, watching her disheveled children play in the field. My aunt sat next to her and listened as the young mother complained about her husband, who failed to provide for their children. "I know that children are a blessing from God, but you have to provide for them," said Aunt Miriam. The woman only muttered something under her breath. My aunt decided to give her a lesson in birth control and asked if she had any wool or cotton. Preferring not to speak, the young mother looked out at the grazing herd beyond the tent. Aunt Miriam advised her to shear the finest wool from one of her lambs, wash it, leave it in the sun to dry, and then put it in a clean bag. The young woman listened with interest. My aunt continued. "When your husband comes to you, take some of the wool, tie it on a string, dip it in olive oil and then insert it in yourself. When he is finished, pull the string out and this will prevent any more children."

I did not fully understand the conversation, but I had an inkling that it was about sex and marveled at my aunt's frankness. She did not think that it was necessary for her to shelter me or my cousin from any subject.

Going back and forth between the village and the farm was always enjoyable. That day was no exception. We mounted our horses and rode to a farm called *Alwadi*. A group of Bedouin men and women working in the fields stopped to greet us. After a brief exchange with the women, my aunt sat with the man in charge and talked about the crops. Similar to other encounters, their conversation quickly turned to laments for bygone days, then to political topics. Their hushed tones and mysterious words made me realize that all was not well in the world. For the first time since my visit, I longed to be with my mother and father. Although my aunt's openness was engaging, and what she instilled in me was enriching, I was often left puzzled. I didn't want to grow up so quickly. I wished that my horse would bolt across the fields and take me back to Nazareth, where I could watch the world unfold, protected by my parents, under the gaze of angels.

I returned to Nazareth when my maternal grandfather's emphysema symptoms worsened. He was experiencing shortness of breath even in a state of rest. Seeing him lying still and without his usual authority was almost as frightening as when he used to look at me disapprovingly. He was strict and took his patriarchal role seriously. He had been a stonecutter for most of his life and spoke repeatedly of the discipline required for the job. His profession had become a symbol of all of life's challenges. Without his physical strength, he often tried to assert his authority, but my grandmother had long since assumed the dominant role and was clearly in charge.

My grandfather's illness affected everyone adversely, except for my grandmother. Confined to his bed, he was unable to make demands on her, and this seemed to lift her spirits. She began to flourish. She spent hours listening to political debates on the radio. Because most of her daughters were still at home, they did the housework, leaving her free to indulge in the pleasures of her grandchildren. As custom required, extended family members and friends came to pay a dutiful visit to my grandfather.

My grandmother's house was not far from where we lived. I spent much of my time there with other relatives who also lived nearby. Because she lived on the main street in Nazareth and her house had a large veranda, neighbors also visited her. I sat with her and watched as she smoked her water pipe in the little garden where my grandfather had spent many days repairing the retaining wall. She taught me the name of every flower, including the cyclamen and red poppies that were native to Galilee, and grew in abundance during the early days of spring, covering the hills around Nazareth.

A man named Abu Ibrahim also visited my grandmother. He was our family doctor. His house calls turned into long visits. Abu Ibrahim was not a real doctor, but he had learned about medicine working as a nurse for an English physician during the British mandate for Palestine. He was good at giving injections and setting bones. He excelled at diagnosing all sorts of illnesses. His gentle manner and toothless smile put his patients at ease. Most people preferred him to a real doctor. He also charged very little, and all pharmacies in Nazareth honored his prescriptions. Those who doubted his skills and went to see a real doctor usually came back to him, having affirmed his diagnoses. None of this changed his character. He retained his modesty, and, because he lived alone, he was always happy when summoned for help.

My only contact with him occurred after dislocating my kneecap from a fall. With one quick move of his hand, my kneecap was back in place, and I was able to accompany my older sisters Najla and Layla to the Sisters of Nazareth convent, where we collected our share of clothes sent to us by American charities. My sisters and I stood by a nun who asked about the size of our family and our ages. After describing our parents to her, she disappeared and then came back with a large bag full of clothes. Unaccustomed to wearing used clothes, my mother was uncomfortable at first, but she eventually set her pride aside. My sisters and I put on our new garments while our mother stood in front of the mirror scrutinizing her own dress. She patted the collar, smoothing the lace around it. She slipped her hand into the front pocket, paused for a second, and then pulled it out. An unclasped pearl necklace dangled from her hand.

Startled, she held it away from her body as though it was a venomous snake, then ordered my sister Najla to take it back to the nuns so it could be returned to its rightful owner. Refusing to extend her hand, my sister had to face our mother's anger. A moral dilemma was suddenly presented to my dispossessed family. Being the head of our household, my father had to arbitrate. He concluded that the necklace was planted in the pocket by a generous donor, then placed it around my mother's neck. My mother's face was transformed—and that put the entire family at ease. I was especially pleased with my new blue shirt and khaki shorts, which I was going to wear the very next day, journeying with my father to his workplace in Haifa.

We were only a few kilometers out of Nazareth when the bus came to a full stop. An Israeli soldier boarded and ordered us to step off the bus. A handful of other soldiers with guns directed us into a straight line and demanded our travel permits. Since all Palestinians were governed by military rules, movement between towns was restricted. A travel permit that had to be renewed frequently was required. After a quick look, those who had valid travel permits were sent back to their seats on the bus. My father was ordered to take off his overcoat. Realizing that this was a regular occurrence, I wondered why he hadn't prepared me for it. My father began to undo the buttons on his coat. Annoyed by his composure, the soldier seized his coat and stripped it off his back with tremendous force.

As I stood next to my father, I recalled how frightened I had been when he once took me to the butcher shop, and I had seen the butcher strip off a lamb's skin, revealing a pink carcass covered in blood and veins. Terrified by the experience, I could not be consoled and had to be taken to my grandmother. She had always been able to soothe me with her own special and thoughtful ways. She led me to her neighbor, who had in her possession a magical vessel known to restore calm to anyone who drank from it. After invoking God's help, my grandmother's friend walked to her glass cabinet and took out a box lined with blue silk, containing a bowl inscribed around its rim with Arabic calligraphy. Placing it on the small table next to me, she poured water into it and asked me to drink. Carefully, I held it up to my mouth and drank every drop. I could feel the water chasing fear away.

Even though I was almost twelve, I still felt fearful standing next to the soldier and wished that I was safe with my grandmother. My father stood motionless. Having experienced incarceration for traveling without a permit soon after the creation of Israel, he was compliant. He had been arrested attempting to return to Haifa soon after our move to Nazareth, in hopes of recovering some of his tools from the bombed-out shop. He disappeared for six months and was presumed dead by my mother, who had to fend for her family on her own. Today, however, he did have a travel permit. Yet, he still looked fearful, and obeyed the soldier's commands without question. We returned to our seats, but my father seemed uncomfortable, and didn't look in my direction. Once everyone was back on the bus, the doors closed, and we resumed our journey. Except for the driver, everyone was Palestinian. Sensing the despair of his passengers, the Jewish driver changed the radio station from the Hebrew broadcast he was listening to. He hoped Arabic music would lighten the mood.

Arriving at the bus station, we were met by Jewish vendors selling unfamiliar goods brought to Haifa from Europe. Eager to start his work, my father took my hand, and we walked away from the busy station. When we arrived at the shop, he greeted his employer in Hebrew and asked me to refer to him as Mr. Moses. I watched my father sharpen his tools on a stone saturated with oil. He pointed to various tools on his bench and sounded out their names in Hebrew. That kept me amused for a while, but soon I became bored. Mr. Moses suggested that perhaps I could accompany him to the hardware store. I pleaded and asked to stay at the shop, but my father insisted. Feeling betrayed, I followed Mr. Moses to a commercial neighborhood near the harbor. As we were trying to cross the street, he took my hand. I remembered my earlier experience at the checkpoint and tried to pull it away, but then realized that this was a moment of human warmth.

When we returned, my father was working on a large shelving unit. He stopped to greet me and then began talking to Mr. Moses. During their conversation, Mr. Moses handed him some money. At the end of the day, we walked back to the bus station, and I could see that my father was happy. With a pocketful of money, he seemed relaxed and more expressive. We entered various shops and bought food. Our last stop was at a flower booth near the bus station where my father bought a large cluster of tulips. As much as I loved their color, I felt slightly uncomfortable when we met the stares of the other Palestinian passengers on the bus ride home. My mother was happy with the food but, like me, uneasy about the idea of having store-bought flowers placed on her dining table while everyone else in the neighborhood was struggling to have food put on theirs.

I was always aware of the discomfort that my mother felt about these small indulgences. I had also seen her alarmed reaction when my aunts yielded to the smallest pleasures when they visited her. My aunts' weekly visits were always a source of joy for me, especially when they read the grounds from the coffee that my mother had served. They would lose themselves in a moment of amusement. Their eyes would light up, then feeling guilty, their laughter would abruptly stop, and they would return to their somber moods.

My mother's jewelry box, which had delighted me in the past with its ballerina that popped out and danced every time it was opened, was no longer on her dressing table. The jewelry had been sold off, and the money was used to pay for the basic necessities of life. The box was now hidden in the closet, containing a few pictures of people whom my mother and father had known in Haifa. These people were no longer in our lives. Banished, they were living as refugees in Lebanon. There was also a picture of a woman named Hadassah, a Jewish woman who lived close to my parents' house before the establishment of Israel. She had come to Palestine from Europe in the early forties, and my parents had befriended her. The jewelry box had become a sad reminder of friendships lost. It lay idle. No one turned the key that wound the music. The ballerina stopped dancing. With the establishment of Israel, the house in Haifa where I was born was no longer ours, it was taken over by a Jewish family. My mother and father never saw Hadassah again. They had unwittingly become enemies, separated not so much by distance, but by their opposing views.

My father pleaded with my mother, asking her to accept the flowers in celebration of his full-time job offer from Mr. Moses. Delighted with the news, my mother put the flowers in a vase and made a feast. I never accompanied my father to work again, choosing instead to remain close to my mother. While my father and my uncles labored under the pressure of the new Israeli rule of Palestine, my grandmother decided to reclaim her sovereignty. Short of raising a flag, she took some security measures and fortified the house by installing a steel gate that separated her house from the street. Inside her small state, my grandmother acted as though she were the president. My grandfather, in ill health, was more like a modern king, only performing ceremonial functions. For these, my grandmother made sure that he dressed appropriately. He wore a *sherwal*, or loose-fitting pants, made with what appeared to be a mile of fabric. Through the wide waist ran an elastic band that was pulled tight around his abdomen. The fabric hung around his body and masked the contours of his figure. Unlike modern pants that showed male shapes and bulges, the *sherwal*, as my grandmother would say, was meant to spare men with small organs the humiliation, and to prevent men with large organs from indulging in foolish pride. My grandmother also made sure that he wore the finest *kumbaz*, a long cream-colored silk gown with gold stripes. Around his waist, he wore a cummerbund, and his crown was a fez—a red hat with a black tassel. With the help of medication, his health improved sufficiently, so that he was able to sit on the veranda and greet passersby.

My grandfather's remission didn't last. He soon returned to his bed and died a short time afterward. My great-uncle Hana was called to verify his death. He was a tall, handsome man whom everyone in the family respected. Until his arrival, we all sat quietly, knowing very well that my grandfather was dead. But we waited for my great-uncle, whom the family held in high regard. When he came into the room, my uncle looked at my grandfather and, without having to examine the body, pronounced him dead.

At these words, everyone broke down and cried. My grandmother fixed her gaze upon my grandfather's motionless body. With tears streaming, her eyes examined his face as though she were seeing him for the first time. His serene face was new to everyone. When alive, my grandfather had been like a volcano, always erupting with anger, or bursting into severe coughing fits due to his emphysema. On the verge of suffocation, his face would redden as he gasped for air, but his pain always failed to elicit my grandmother's sympathy. Instead, I saw anger and resentment on her face. Her reaction to his death seemed sincere. She moved toward him and began to stroke his head. This sudden and unaccustomed display of affection surprised everyone. She spoke to his lifeless body and seemed surprised at what she now perceived to be his sudden death.

My great-uncle, her brother, pulled her away. He ordered hot water and a shaving kit. Then he began to shave my grandfather. The razor blade moved quickly across his face. Knowing that he couldn't hurt the lifeless body, my uncle moved with great confidence and speed. Still too young to fear death, I stood there observing a sad event from a safe distance. My grandfather was buried the next day. A Roman Catholic priest led his funeral procession, followed by a group of scouts who beat drums. Behind them came the mourners and young men who took turns carrying the coffin on their shoulders.

It was the custom for people who had lost a loved one to remain at home for forty days. During this period of mourning, the family of the deceased would receive condolences. My grandmother had not left her house in a long time. She was comfortable in her own home and garden. Although she had never shown affection for my grandfather when he was alive, she had never shrugged off her responsibility to him and rarely stepped out of her door to seek company. Rather, extended family and friends came to visit her. For the next forty days, she remained at home and received mourners.

Because her house was in a prominent location on the main street, many friends and relatives who were on their way to the market stopped for a brief visit. Even Yossi, the Iraqi Jewish photographer, and Jacob, the Romanian street-clothes vendor, found shelter from the heat in her backyard and would often come in for a glass of water, but also to promote their business. Jacob used to carry his merchandise in large suitcases and would often be drenched in sweat as he struggled with their heavy weight. However, with the advice of my grandmother, he abandoned the cases and began to carry the clothes like an Arab merchant, in a huge cloth bundle. He would often say that it was easier on his back, and, in his very limited and broken Arabic, he would add, "The Arab way is the better way."

That pleased my grandmother to no end. She knew that there was a lot of tension in Arab-Jewish relations. The struggle for survival was a fierce one, but she saw the vendors as individuals. Jacob lived in Upper Nazareth, a place of rare natural beauty, high on the hills, and overlooking the historical town. The new Upper Nazareth had been built in haste to house Eastern European Jews. It was a lonely place in those early days, and Jacob spent most of his time in Old Nazareth doing business with Palestinians and peddling his trinkets, which he carried in a separate small bundle to Christian pilgrims.

Yossi recognized my grandmother's importance in her neighborhood and wanted desperately to capture her in a photograph. To his dismay, she always refused, fearing that it would be an act of vanity. He said to her that if she agreed, then others in the neighborhood would do the same and pay him to have theirs taken. In time, she began to feel as if she was preventing him from making a living, and finally agreed.

I watched as he mounted his large camera on top of the wooden tripod and then draped it in a black curtain. When he was ready, he placed a chair in front of the white screen and turned around, only to discover that she was still sitting on the low bench by the window. Surprised, he asked if she was going to get ready. She was. She met all events in her life with the same simple dresses. Realizing that she was not going to change, he sat her on a chair, and, in the mistaken belief that his profession allowed him the liberty, he began to stroke and adjust her hair with a familiarity that made her visibly uncomfortable. It wasn't until he had vanished behind the camera skirt that she relaxed her face. At that moment, the flash went off. He re-emerged from behind the camera's skirt looking triumphant.

When he returned the following week, everyone in the room waited in anticipation to see the picture. Opening his case, Yossi removed a brown envelope. Sensing our eagerness, he didn't reveal the photo. Instead, he proceeded to talk about the art of photography in classical, formal Arabic instead of ordinary speech. This dramatic expression astounded everyone in the room. Yet, we could see that it was part of the drama he wanted to create before revealing the photograph. This was his finest moment. He knew that if people liked her picture, he would be hired to take many more photographs in the neighborhood.

My grandmother looked at her image with obvious pleasure, but did not lose her composure. Then she looked at

Yossi and said, "May God bless your hands. You did a good job." Beaming, Yossi reverted to his colloquial Arabic, which he could speak more quickly.

Whenever Yossi and Jacob met at my grandparents' house, Jacob would avoid speaking to him. Although both men were Jewish, their common religion wasn't enough to make them the same. Yossi, born in Iraq to a family that had lived there for many generations, was more like an Arab. He could converse with my grandmother with ease. He also had a flamboyant personality, which seemed to intimidate Jacob, who would retreat to a corner.

Leaving my grandmother's house that day, I decided to walk home through the market, where there was much to explore within its walls and alleys that divided the sections. The fruit and vegetables were in one area. From there I could wander into the metal market and see the coppersmiths at work. They would break into sweat, even in mid-winter, as they pumped air into the coal oven. Their arm muscles swelled with the motion of moving the wooden lever up and down with great speed, while the metal turned to amber red. I watched in wonder as other men took out the hot and pliable material and shaped it into tools and kitchen utensils.

The workmen didn't object to children watching, so long as they wished them good health. This was a courtesy that I had learned from my grandfather. He taught me to never walk by working men without saying, "*Allah yatic al-afya*," "May God give you strength and good health." This had endeared me to everyone except the coffin maker. He simply ignored me and continued to focus on his large electric table saw. I repeated my greeting in a louder voice. He finally turned his machine off and approached me waving an extended fingerless hand. "Look at my hand!" he shouted. "Do you know why I have no fingers?" I was scared but couldn't run away. "I have no fingers because I am a modern man, using modern machines, and people like you distract me with their stupid superstitions!" Terrified, I apologized and walked back to the fruit and vegetable section of the market, fought my way through the crowds, and took the long way home.

The market was always a place of intense drama. It was there that I first noticed the men who were called *majanin,* "the insane." Of these, I most admired Al-Ousta, a tall and muscular man with a big beard and long tangled hair. He was intensely nervous and never acknowledged people around him or returned their greeting. Yet, despite his wild appearance, he possessed the qualities of an educated man. He wrote verses on pieces of cardboard and his style of calligraphy was superior to that of any of my teachers. He also possessed a beautiful voice. Al-Ousta didn't sing to anyone in particular. He always cupped his hand over one ear to channel his voice directly into his head for his own pleasure. I often watched him from a short distance as he crafted his next verse. As soon as one was complete, he would place it next to him on the stone step where he was seated, stare at it for a while, and then place it in his coat pocket. Watching him, I noticed that many people placed money next to him, and that he seemed to have more money than the working men and women who toiled in the market. It was a revelation to discover that goods and services were not the only thing that people paid for.

I had seen men standing on street corners without goods or tools, offering to read the fortune of those with predictable destinies. Observing these fortune tellers, I decided that selling nothing was possible, but there was a trick to it. It obviously required a special mind like that of Al-Ousta, who made more money than anyone else in the market. Strangely, he didn't seem to have any use for it. He always wore the same tattered clothes and lived in a cave just on the edge of town, not far from my grandmother's house.

I once told my grandmother about Al-Ousta and about how he was not making any use of his money. She said that this was often the case. "It's one of those ironies of life," she explained. "God often gives meat to people without teeth."

Al-Ousta was not one of us. He was different in every way. He didn't speak our Arabic, but Egyptian Arabic, which we were mostly able to understand. No one could comprehend how an Egyptian man ended up on the streets of Nazareth. Rumors about Al-Ousta circulated. Many believed the unlikely story that he was an Egyptian pilot who'd been shot down during the Egyptian air raids on Tel Aviv in 1948 and had somehow escaped and found his way into Nazareth.

The market also had coffeehouses. Old men spent their days sitting there and playing backgammon, and young men also frequented them. One of these young men was my brother-in-law George, who was married to my sister Najla. Thanks to him, I was allowed inside such places. He believed that I brought him good luck. He won his backgammon match almost every time he took me with him. Men from all walks of life, including teachers, poets, and politicians, mingled with laborers and street vendors there. Listening to the different conversations, I felt inspired, and wished that I could spend the weekdays with George and learn from the men there, instead of being confined to my hard wooden chair and desk at school.

My dislike for school stemmed from the sense of detachment and isolation that I felt in the classroom. The French Brothers, my teachers, were stern and contemptuous of anything that was outside their set of beliefs or norms. I was also different from the others in my class. My acute asthma and inability to pronounce certain letters in Arabic because of a lisp made me feel deeply ashamed, especially when my Rs turned into Vs, a sound only associated with foreign words. Whenever I was required to read aloud, an uproar of laughter would erupt in the classroom. Gradually, I developed an irrational fear of reading, and my capacity for writing diminished. I began to skip school, going instead up to the hills around Nazareth and spending my day drifting through the woods. There, I met boys shepherding their flocks and listened as they played their flutes. Other times, when I wanted to be alone, I would go to the English cemetery and hide among the graves. Since Britain was out of Palestine, the steel gates were always locked, and the high walls surrounding it made for the perfect hideout. After climbing the gates, I would jump in and spend the day exploring the headstones with names so different from my own.

Without maintenance, flowers that had once been controlled turned wild, flowering, flourishing, and covering much of the ground. It was a perfect place. I would sit there and daydream while soaking up the gentle winter sunlight. Because most people in Nazareth were superstitious, the cemetery became my own. Looking at the inscriptions on the gravestones, I tried to imagine the people who were buried under them. It saddened me that no one ever came to invoke their shared memories with their dead. I wanted to rush home and tell my mother about my hiding place but feared that she would be angry with me for skipping school and tell my father.

Burdened with guilt, I decided instead to tell my grandmother about skipping school, and about my feelings of sadness for the dead Englishmen and women who were buried far away from home. I knew that I could trust her to keep the secret. She would surely understand, for it was she who instilled those feelings of compassion in me. I so often heard her talk about her cousin who had gone to South America in a time when migration was extremely rare. She would lament the separation from his family and friends and spoke of the day when his bones would forever rest in foreign soil. I wanted to run and tell her right away, but her house was always full of visitors. The end of the day would be the only time where I might find her alone on the little mat in the garden, smoking her water pipe.

When I did finally arrive, my grandmother was there just as I had expected. After greeting her I sat on the mat and didn't look in her direction. Sensing that I was there to tell her something, she waited for me to start. But because I was nervous, I just sat there listening to the gurgling sound of the water in her pipe. Realizing that I was reluctant to speak, she looked at me and asked, "Do you have something to tell me?" Encouraged by the tone in her voice, I finally said that I didn't like school, and confessed to skipping some of my classes. Emboldened by her lack of reaction, I told her about my hiding place in the English cemetery. Clearly uncomfortable, she asked, "How do you enter a cemetery that has been bolted and secured with heavy chains for as long as I can remember?"

Unaccustomed to displaying anger before me, she turned her face away and puffed on the pipe vigorously, causing the bubbles in the water to rage on her behalf.

I knew that she was unhappy with me but didn't know how to convey her feelings about it. She had very little education herself and wasn't sure of the values offered at school. I felt uneasy about confiding in her but was consoled when she said that she still loved me. My grandmother's kind words brought me back to her. I had been spending so much time at the market that I had forgotten how nice it was to be with her.

The Brides

My maternal uncles, Jamil and his younger brother Afif, were nearing the age of marriage. They were still single, despite their good looks and fairly successful business. Their car repair shop was one of the few in Nazareth. Anxious about their lack of interest in marriage, my grandmother vowed to find them brides. She decided to line up ten girls for them to choose from. I remember watching as she scrubbed the cement floor in the courtyard. I helped her set up the special outdoor reception area. We placed a large straw mat on the floor and positioned soft cushions on it. The portable clay fire burner was placed near the seating arrangement, and, although the fire was small, one could still feel the heat. My grandmother was fond of the coal burner in the winter, but on that summer day, she sat a good distance from it. The burner was needed for boiling coffee and to light the tobacco in the water pipe.

When my great-grandmother arrived, everyone stood up until she was comfortably seated on the cushions. She looked like no one else in our family, having lived for so long. She was from a different era. Her face was tattooed, and she wore long, dark, traditional clothing. Resuming their seats, the others sat next to her according to their rank, based on age alone. My grandmother sat to her right, wearing her usual simple loose-fitting dress, but to acknowledge the occasion, she put on a colorful embroidered headscarf. Being the oldest of her sisters, my mother sat on her left, dressed in the latest European fashion of the day and with nothing on her head. With the utmost humility, my grandmother addressed her mother and asked her to bless the event. My grandmother then solicited the help of everyone present in finding brides for my uncles.

From among the women gathered came the names of ten families with suitable girls. My aunts would visit one such family every week and each would have a task to perform. One aunt would engage the potential bride in conversation, checking her intellect, while another would check her posture as she walked. Engaging her in a whisper would check her hearing, but the most difficult task was given to my aunt Wardi, who would check her eyes. Wardi brought the smallest needle that she could find. The first girl failed miserably when asked to thread the needle by Aunt Wardi, who sat there with the embroidery on her lap pretending to be too old to see the needle properly. The visit to the second family did not yield much better results, despite the fact that the girl was able to thread the needle with ease and had good looks. My youngest aunt complained that although the potential bride had a beautiful face, the expression on it seemed locked in an unpleasant pose, as if she just had a whiff of someone passing wind. All of the others failed as well. My aunts decided that a new strategy was needed.

Many months went by. At no time had my uncles shown the slightest interest in the matter. My grandmother decided that it was time to consult with people who could break spells. This was not the first time that this had been considered to aid in the marriage of my uncles. My grandfather once dug a section of the path leading to his house on the advice of a sorcerer, who suspected that the written spell was buried there, yet the spell was never found. My grandmother believed that as long as her sons continued to walk on the pathway where the spell was buried, they would remain single. She could not understand why her two young and good-looking sons were not interested in marriage and concluded that their lack of interest was due to sorcery.

My grandmother decided that it was time to dig in the pathway again. Under her supervision, everyone dug and sifted through the earth like skilled archaeologists. When something was found, it was inspected and put aside. Most of the objects were articles of glass or fabric, and might have been of historical significance to someone, but they were worthless to the people who were in search of a certain piece of paper. Finally, it was unearthed. The paper was small and recognized by everyone as relatively new. The writing on it was beyond recognition, but my grandmother at once believed it was the spell.

After disposing of it in the coal burner, we watched as the fire engulfed the small piece of paper, and I could see the relief on my grandmother's face. Though my uncles did not believe in magic spells, digging up the path sent them a strong signal, and they understood that it was time to get married. Within months, they had found their own brides and were engaged to women with facial expressions that satisfied my youngest aunt, who declared that the brides must have been raised in fragrant rose gardens. One year later, they were both married. My grandmother soon had more grandchildren sharing her house, and her life became busy again.

I continued to visit her, but quickly understood that my role had changed when she began to ask for my help with small tasks, such as going to the store for her. Upon my return, she would put my head on her lap and squirt salt water in my ears, as she believed it prevented a heat stroke. And even that ritual came to an end when one day she said to me, "You don't need salt water anymore. May God protect you; you have become a strong young man."

Even though I was almost fifteen, I wasn't ready to be a young man. I was happy to be a boy, protected by my mother and my father. Being a man meant that I would have to venture out into the larger society and face the kind of hostility and interrogation that my father did at the checkpoint.

A few years later, after my sixteenth birthday, my father took me to Haifa. Through his employer I was introduced to a builder, who hired me as a laborer on his construction site. Unlike Nazareth, where Arabic was the only language spoken among its inhabitants, many languages were spoken in Haifa—German, Polish, Russian, Romanian, Hungarian, and Arabic. But it was the North African Arabic spoken by the Moroccan Jews, not the Arabic spoken in Palestine. The official language was Hebrew, but most workers preferred their own language. Many spoke Yiddish. It was during the lunch hour that I first encountered segregation. The Jewish workers sat around tables in one area, while the Palestinian workers, who made the wooden forms that shaped the tall buildings, sat on cinderblocks. Haifa, the city where my mother spent her youth, and had loved so much, no longer looked the same. Although the new buildings were largely built by exploited Palestinian workers, they stood as a modern symbols of civility.

My favorite place in Haifa was Hadar Hacarmel, an upscale neighborhood where I often went to see movies after work. It was there that I discovered a new genre of film. Unlike the Nazareth movie house, where the choice was always limited to one film, Haifa had many different theatres and films to choose from. I saw *Rebel Without a Cause*, *West Side Story*, *Irma la Douce* with Shirley MacLaine, and *To Sir, with Love* with Sidney Poitier. I was so inspired by the dignity of Poitier's character that I dared to imagine another life for myself.

Working with people who only thought of me as an Arab boy unworthy of their kindness and respect made me angry. I wished that I could tell my Jewish co-workers who I really was. I wanted to tell them about my father's knowledge of literature and his creativity, about my grandfather's healing skills and the sweetness of his voice, for he was a cantor at the Greek Melkite Catholic church in his village. I wanted to tell them that I had a wonderful and loving family, capable of great feeling—a family who had held their grace in the face of the poverty and the demeaning hostility of everyday life, brought upon them since the creation of Israel. Yet I knew that it was only a matter of time before civility would be lost, and my suppressed anger would come to the surface. Still, I held on to optimism. In fact, I was making a breakthrough with one German Jewish worker named Dov, who chose me as his helper. Our conversation was mostly limited to work matters, except on one occasion when he asked if I had a father. Then, with the same breath, he asked if we had a radio at home. Oddly, other Jewish workers had asked me the same question, yet I never understood the significance. As luck would have it, I was able to answer both questions and said, "Yes, I have a father who makes radios in his spare time for a company in Haifa." My answer surprised him. He asked if my father was an electrical engineer. I told him no, but explained that he was a carpenter and cabinetmaker, and that he made radio cases from beautiful wood, and then polished them with the finest French polish. I described how my mother helped my father stretch the fabric on the case, where the speaker would be installed.

Dov smiled and said that the case wasn't a radio until the electrical components were installed in it. I had to agree with him, but explained how I used to put my head inside the case when I was a young boy, before reciting the stories from *The Arabian Nights* for my brothers and my sisters. Dov smiled again. His blue eyes carefully examined my face. He didn't tell me much about himself, but I could tell from his curiosity about my family that he was interested in other cultures. I told him more stories about my father and paternal grandfather. He was especially interested in my grandfather's singing. He expressed his own love for sacred music. I was also curious about his country of birth and wanted to know about his past, but I hoped that one day he would tell me voluntarily. However, he never told me anything about himself. He only continued to inquire about my life.

Dov and I worked together for over a year. One day, he failed to come to work, and I was assigned to help another man with mixing lime for the painters. Mixing lime was not an easy job. I had to mix the corrosive substance and then deliver buckets to the different floors of apartment buildings. It was backbreaking work, and never appreciated by anyone. I eventually became fearful and weighed down with feelings of hopelessness at work. It was not until I returned to Nazareth and to my friends that I felt whole again. My friends and I spent many hours talking about our bleak futures and the limits of our aspirations. We were eager to explore our country but were not allowed to. Imposed martial law continued to make travel without a permit illegal for Palestinian citizens. And yet, this pseudo-democracy still managed to win the admiration of the free world.

As I grew older, I began to fear that living under such demeaning conditions would result in hatred. I tried hard to maintain a balance between my gentle self and my anger. Because I couldn't lash out at my Israeli coworkers, I would sometimes vent my anger on my family and friends. Of course, I was not the only one behaving this way. Without legal protection, we were forced into total submission, and we began to accept and even inhabit the negative Israeli perception of us. I tried to lessen their hostility by conforming to the culture of the Israelis. I bought my clothes in Haifa and adopted some Israeli speech patterns, thinking it might win me their acceptance and ease my workday. I worked very hard on mastering my Hebrew, and my conversational command was superior to that of many Jewish workers, who still preferred to speak Yiddish.

My father fared better than me in Haifa. His cabinet-making skills and his mastery in restoring antiques were highly sought after. Having no such skills to offer, I was

135

replaceable. Although my mother and father had done their best to nurture fine qualities in me, anger would sometimes take over, and I would have a lapse of judgment, or behave offensively toward my family and friends. Hating your oppressor is a great temptation, but I managed not to give into those feelings for a very long time. To vent my anger, I attempted to write resistance poetry, but I lacked talent. This was not an original idea. I was merely trying to emulate real poets, such as Mahmoud Darwish, who was only a few years older than me. He had already achieved a high literary status and was inspiring other poets to resist the oppressive Israeli laws. I was restless though, and wanted immediate relief from the restrictions that we were under. I began to think about illegally crossing the border into Lebanon or Jordan, as many young men had done. In order to cross the border, I would have to walk at night in the wilderness and risk being shot. Even if I had a successful crossing, I would never be able to return, and be condemned to live my life without family and friends.

I had witnessed the pain and sadness of those who were left behind. One of my older cousins had escaped to Jordan. He left a note for his family informing them of his departure and was never seen again. That experience had shaken both the family and everyone else in the neighborhood. His mother and father were devastated by the loss. They had no idea where he was or even whether he was dead or alive. I recalled my mother and father's anguish over his departure, and here I was planning to do the same. I couldn't stand the idea of never seeing my parents again. Still, my desire to flee remained, and I continued planning my escape even though I doubted I was strong enough to do it.

My plans were put on hold when a relative and I traveled on the bus to Nesher, a town near Haifa, to meet with my new Hungarian employer. Yaakov was a strong looking man with a kind and cheerful personality, and a warm handshake. I soon discovered that he was a Holocaust survivor—when he rolled up his sleeve to mix lime for paint in a deep bucket, I saw a number tattooed on his arm. Working with him was easy. He was respectful and kind. I worked hard to please him. Sometimes our work took us far beyond his town, and I sat behind him with my arms wrapped around his waist, as his old Vespa sped down the highway. His tolerant attitude toward me served as an example to his clients. Many of them were from Hungary and other parts of Europe, and I was eventually treated with respect. I was even befriended by one family, who took interest in me, and they came to visit me in Nazareth.

Working for Yaakov allowed me to be at peace with myself. This was very different from my situation on the large construction site, where I found all of my encounters to be challenging and difficult. I became less angry and started to map out a different plan. Instead of crossing to Jordan or Lebanon, I would emigrate to another country. My grand-mother's Armenian neighbor and his family had just left Nazareth and immigrated to Montreal. I hoped to do the same and began to gather information about Canada.

Six months after their departure, my grandmother re-ceived a letter from Montreal, which contained a picture of her neighbors standing next to a blue American car. Motivated by their success, I took driving lessons. My instructor was a large man named Abraham. He had a big mustache, and his spoken Hebrew was peppered with Yiddish and Polish. He even spoke a few words in Arabic. He never called me by my name but instead "*ya habibi*," Arabic for "my love," a common term of endearment usually used among friends. Languages were merging. Arabs began to use Hebrew in their everyday speech, and Jews were using Arabic expressions.

I decided to buy a used car soon after receiving my license. My search led me to a young man in Nazareth who was leaving the country in a few weeks and going to Vancouver. I mentioned that I was planning to go to Montreal, but didn't know how to initiate the process, and asked if he could help me. To my surprise, he had an extra application form in his house and gave it to me, telling me that I could apply for emigration to Canada whenever I was ready. The next day, we drove to Haifa to change his car's ownership to my name. Having the form made me happy. It gave me a sense of control. But it was also a sad reminder that I would be separating from my family and home.

I gave myself a year to save enough money for travel expenses, as I was told it would take that long to complete the process. I continued to work hard and didn't go out to see my friends as often as I used to. I began to study my mother's face as she sat on the balcony. I wanted to make sure that I would never forget the way she looked, no matter how great the distance was between us. My mother seemed to be aware of what I was doing. I had the feeling that she was discreetly doing the same thing when I was reading. Out of the corner of my eye, I would catch her looking at me.

I made frequent visits to my father's small shop in Nazareth. He kept his tools there and made small pieces of furniture that he sold on Saturday, his day off. I loved the smell of wood shavings and shellac that I associated with his scent. These visits became an attempt at getting to know my father more. I desperately wanted to get to know him better before I left. I also hoped that he would say something that would convince me to stay, that he would tell me a solution to our struggles was just around the corner, that he would give me hope for a better future. But he never did.

I didn't need to examine my father's features the way I examined my mother's. He was easy to remember. His dark eyes were set deep in his face, which was covered with pockmarks caused by a childhood illness. I wanted to tell him how sorry I was for not making more of an effort to get to know him better. I wanted to tell him how much I loved him. But that was not something that men did in those days.

Leaving home proved to be more difficult than I had anticipated. I still didn't have enough money for my airplane ticket or living expenses. Then I discovered that my younger brother Souheil, who was attending the same French Catholic School that I had gone to, was buying a travel case for a trip to France in order to study theology. Unlike me, he had become so involved with the Christian Brothers from France that he prayed with them, ate with them, and didn't come home until all his homework was completed. He admired their lifestyle and wanted to become a Brother himself.

The Lasallian Order was going to pay for his studies abroad and for all the other expenses. While my parents objected to my plans to leave home, they were happy with my brother's plan. In fact, my mother and father were very pleased at the prospect of having a son with a university degree. I was also happy for him and knew he would be coming back home after four years, since he had been promised a teaching position at his school in Nazareth. My own wish was much harder to fulfill. Knowing how painful it would be for my parents if two of their sons left in same year, I decided to put my future plans on hold so as to allow my brother to leave and fulfill my parents' dream.

The Six Day War

The simmering tension between Israel and its neighbors since its inception in 1948 had once again erupted in late May 1967. The looming signs of war appeared when tanks loaded on trucks rolled through the streets of Nazareth. My friends and I, anxious about what might come next, gathered nightly in a coffeehouse with the only television set in town and watched the news. We didn't feel the total despair that our fathers felt. We were young, and believed that the neighboring Arab states would soon come to our aid and restore what had been taken away from us by force, and that everyone would return to their homes. Unlike our fathers, who had a deeper understanding of politics, my friends and I, along with millions of other young men and women throughout the Middle East, were under the spell of the charismatic Egyptian leader, Gamal Abdel Nasser. We embraced the unattainable dream of Arab unity and the conceit which often comes with nationalism.

I sat on the rocky hills around Nazareth with my friends, discussing topics that were bigger than we were and that we didn't fully understand. Our knowledge of history was limited. Although Israel had banned the teaching of Palestinian history in schools, few of us felt the need to prove our right to live on our forefathers' land where we were born. The whole argument about to whom the land belonged seemed utterly absurd to us. Nevertheless, the Israelis had managed to cast doubt in our minds about our right to live in a country that had always been our own.

Although justice for my family and community was of great importance to me, I had many competing interests. I was young and wanted to explore the world. I was still living under the spell of my Great Aunt Wardi's stories. A childless woman, she could not live on her own after the death of her husband, so she moved in with her brother (my grandfather) and his family and stayed there until her death. She had immersed herself in her own particular form of artistry. Her needlework was highly admired and sold in the finest souvenir shops in Nazareth. However, she remained modest and said very little, even when relatives came to visit. She would sit on the veranda for hours, watching people go by. Suitably joyless and sad, she set a model example for other widows and lived as her society expected of her. I liked her fondness for simple things. I often sat with her to watch the animals that walked down the street below us. Her interest in the caravans was not lost on the man driving the camels. He would often stop to ask her for a glass of water.

Aunt Wardi was also the one who came to my rescue when I was a young boy. I had once wandered out to the hills behind my grandmother's house, where the cactus pears grew. Tempted by their beautiful color, I decided to pick some for my grandmother. In doing so, I ended up with small thorns embedded everywhere in my body and blistered skin. I ran crying to my grandmother, who tried to pick them out with tweezers, but I was covered with the painful thorns. Aunt

Wardi could do her needlework while looking away. As she observed people and events in her vicinity, her tablecloths grew in size, and the precision of her patterns never strayed. Seeing my grandmother struggle with the thorns, she asked me to sit with her. To distract me from discomfort, she told me stories until the caravan finally appeared in the distance. She went down to the street. The man, seeing my great aunt with a cup in her hand, thought that she was there to bring him water. He approached her with an air of excited confidence, only to discover that she wanted camel saliva. The man obliged her, scraping some from around the camel's mouth. This was easy, as camels salivated regularly. Soon, she was back with the drool. She told me that she was going to spread it on my body. I resisted until she explained that it was the only thing that could dissolve the tiny thorns embedded in my skin. "Haven't you seen camels eat thorny cactus leaves?" she asked me. I nodded my head, and she assured me that the saliva was going to melt all the thorns away. I closed my eyes as she rubbed the slimy substance on my body. It wasn't long before the thorns were gone.

In gratitude, Aunt Wardi was invited to our house for a whole week. I sat with her on the mat as she did her needlework. Blue veins visible through the transparent skin on her hands formed patterns as intricate as her needlework. I watched as she transformed a spool of yarn into very elaborate patterns and designs. Mostly, I remembered her tales, and how different they were from the ones I'd heard before. Aunt Wardi's stories were never about a prince who was in pursuit of the most beautiful princess, or about men seeking fortunes. Hers were about men who traveled to faraway places, and across the seven seas in search of knowledge, who did not return until they had reached a higher state of consciousness. I didn't fully understand the morals of her stories at the time, but whether I knew it or not, Aunt Wardi's colorful tales were introducing me to a new and abstract way of thinking.

One day, I came to realize how much influence her stories had on me, when I found myself looking at the world atlas and trying to figure out how many seas were between Nazareth and Canada.

The regular flow of military vehicles through Nazareth in early June of 1967 was a clear sign that war between Israel and its neighbors was imminent. Recognizing the gravity of the situation, my previous excitement about seeing justice restored ended, and was replaced by terrible fear. Many of my friends stopped going to work, but I decided to check with my employer first. Yaakov was not in his work overalls when I arrived at his house. He was wearing a military uniform. I approached him cautiously, fearing that the heated rhetoric between the warring factions was also raging in his heart. Sensing my reluctance, he welcomed me with his usual pleasant manner. "*Boker tov*," he greeted me, Hebrew for "good morning." I echoed back his greeting, inwardly doubting that it was going to be a good morning. I imagined that one of us would be dead by the end of this war.

Being a gentleman, he invited me into his home for coffee and told me that work had been put on hold, as all military reservists had been called for service. We sat in the kitchen glancing at each other but said very little. Trying to relieve the awkward silence, he excused himself to another room and came back with money in his hand. He paid me but didn't mention any future work. Not knowing the outcome of the war, he simply thanked me for being a good worker. I put the money in my pocket and quickly stood up, wished him good luck, and left. Afterward, I felt like a traitor. Why had I said that? Wishing him luck meant wishing for the defeat for our liberators. Yet I could not help but remember his kindness. I wished that I didn't have to confront these conflicting emotions so early in my life.

To intimidate the Palestinian inhabitants in Nazareth, Israeli warplanes flew overhead, deploying their sonic booms, which sounded like huge explosions. The market, which was friendly and civil most of the time, became inhospitable. My friends and I stopped going there. We began to congregate in a small tailor's shop owned by my older friend Nikoula, whom I had periodically assisted in the hopes of learning his trade. We sat there from morning to the end of the day, drinking coffee and listening to the radio. We kept switching between stations, from Voice of Israel to Sawt al-Arab, Voice of the Arabs, from Egypt. We also listened to BBC, my grandfather's most trusted source of news. Despite our fear, my friends and I felt restless. We didn't wish for an endless standstill. We wanted the war to start.

On June 5, 1967, the war did start. I left the tailor's shop and rushed home to see my family, but my mother was the only one there. Unaware of what was happening, she simply carried on with her usual routine. When I told her that the war had started, she said that she was busy having her own war with a huge load of laundry. Soon, my father came home and told us to pack lightly, as we were going to stay with my sister Najla —not in her house, but in her husband's storage room. He was a food merchant, and his shop was located beyond the narrow streets of the old market in Nazareth, where cars and tanks couldn't travel. We gathered there with my sister and her children. That same day, my grandmother and her family also came to stay with us, as their house was on the main road, which was heavily trafficked by Israeli military vehicles.

The storage room was large and had thick walls that gave the illusion of safety to those unfamiliar with the destructive power of modern weaponry. After organizing the food supplies, we huddled around the radio and listened to different stations broadcasting from countries that were involved in the conflict. Yet none of the reports seemed credible. All of the warring factions made claims of victory. Trying to get a sense of what was happening, the adults went up to the roof at night and listened to the sounds of explosions in the distance. Having grown accustomed to the sound, we were no longer gripped by fear. We stood watching the Israeli helicopters as they flew back and forth from the Syrian front.

On the sixth day, the Israeli radio announced a total victory over all the Arab armies, and on behalf of the government asked everyone to resume their normal activities. We moved out of the storage room and my mother returned to her laundry. For several days, I sat at home in a state of shock and disbelief. The Jordanian army had been driven out of the West Bank, and Egypt had been driven out of Gaza, leaving Israel in control of all the Palestinian territories, as well as the Golan Heights in Syria and the Sinai Desert in Egypt. I realized that Israel was not the vulnerable state that it had claimed to be. With the support of most Western countries, Israel knew exactly what the outcome would be. For the first time, I was able to feel the despair that my father and men of his generation had felt all along.

After sitting at home for a few days, I decided that it was time for me to seriously consider leaving the country. My brother Souheil had changed his mind one night about going to France. His decision made it easier for me to leave. I filled in the form that I still had in my dresser drawer and sent it to the Canadian Embassy in Tel Aviv. After eight months of hard work, I saved enough money for my travel expenses. In January 1968, I received an acceptance letter from the embassy, followed by another one a few weeks later requesting my attendance for the required medical exams.

Not long after the war, I lay naked on an exam table in Tel Aviv, feeling vulnerable and utterly dispossessed. After I was checked from head to toe, the doctor declared that I was fit to emigrate. Two months later, I was summoned back to the Canadian Embassy for a brief meeting, then given an envelope containing my visa and immigration documents.

The news was not received well. My entire family made a final attempt to dissuade me from leaving, and my friends and neighbors tried to do the same. The idea of me leaving the country was as new to them as it was to me, but I was committed to my plan and bought a plane ticket.

It was only then that I realized the enormity of my decision. My close friends gave me a going-away party that lasted well into the night. I could tell that my departure was causing an emotional strain on everyone in the room. The next day, I drove to see my relatives in Shefa-'Amr for a final farewell, making sure that my last stop would be my Aunt Miriam's house. We talked about the old days when I was a young boy, and about riding horses on her farm. My aunt no longer farmed or had any animals. Her sons, unable to compete with the modern methods of large-scale Israeli farming, stopped after their father's death and joined the labor force. When my visit was over, she held me tightly and wept.

My heart ached driving home and, remembering the happy times I'd had on my aunt's farm, I found myself thinking about the boy who had lived next door to her house. I remembered how he was mercilessly teased about the hump on his back. I reflected on the bond that we had developed and the joy we felt being with one another. I thought about the day he took me to the hills to see a dead donkey that had fallen into a deep crevice. The stench of the decay had been so horrible that I ran away until I couldn't run anymore, then waited until he caught up with me. He asked if I wanted to feel the hump on his back. I put my hand on it without knowing just how long I ought to leave it there. Without looking at me, he asked if it was disgusting. I said that it wasn't.

Our house was full of people when I returned. The young people wished that they were leaving the country too, but the old men could not understand why I wanted to leave my country, family, and friends. Two days before my departure, I went to say goodbye to the few Jewish friends I had who lived around Nazareth. My first visit was to a family that lived only a short distance from Nazareth. My relationship with the couple there was built on mutual affection. Although we had opposing views on politics, they allowed me to state my own freely and without fear. They were also among the few Jewish friends who came to visit my home and my family with their daughters. My next visit was to my employer, Yaakov, who seemed sad to see me leave when we parted company. I was glad that he had managed to come home from the war in one piece. My last stop was Haifa, my birthplace. While there, I decided to look in on an old Jewish woman for whom my brother and I had done work for. We cleaned and maintained her garden, painted her walls, even went to the store for her. She had been kind and fed us lunch every time we did work for her. After telling her about my planned departure, she took my hand and held it as firmly as an old woman could and said that she was going to miss my help.

When I was back in Nazareth, a military vehicle stopped near our backyard. Alarmed, I stood by the window and saw a high-ranking member of the Israeli Air Force walking toward our house. I recognized him as the son of the very woman I had just visited in Haifa. Not wanting the neighbors to think that I had dealings with the Israeli military, I quickly ran outside to the open yard before he could make it to our house and asked him if everything was all right with his mother.

"My mother is fine," he answered. "I was just at her place, and she informed me of your departure. I decided to come here to say thank you for being kind to her, but also to wish you a good and happy life in Canada."

Sensing that his visit was causing alarm in the neighborhood, he placed his hand on my shoulder to indicate to people watching from their windows that this was a friendly visit.

After he left, everyone wanted to know where I had met such a man. They wondered why a high-ranking air force captain would bother with me. I asked myself the same question. Why had he come? Had there been a hidden reason for his visit? My father, who had witnessed the interaction, said that the man had already stated his reason. He told me not to worry about what people might say.

On my final day at home, old women from the neighborhood came to visit me. They brought amulets with them and asked God to give me blessings and safety. They had sewn their written prayers inside small fabric pouches, which they attached to a string that formed a necklace. Grateful, I lowered my head as they placed them around my neck. Decked with good luck charms, I thanked them and tucked the amulets into my shirt. I watched as the atmosphere in our house fluctuated between that of a wedding and that of a wake.

Aware that it was going to be the last time that I would fall asleep surrounded by my family, I went to bed savoring my remaining hours at home. The next morning, a taxi came to pick me up. I left, accompanied by my mother and father, and all my siblings. As we drove through the main street, we were intercepted by my grandmother and all my aunts and uncles who lived directly across from my grandmother's house. After embracing everyone, we returned to the taxi and drove off. Surrendering to the certainty of my departure, my family and I sat quietly in the taxi and didn't say much until our arrival at Ben Gurion Airport. After checking my suitcase at the counter, I was asked to follow a security personnel, who directed me to a small room for questioning. My family and I said our goodbyes in haste. It was then that I saw my father cry for the first time. No one else dared to cry. My father's tears sufficed for everyone.

As I waited to board my plane, my thoughts were on the future, yet no matter how hard I tried, I could not imagine what was on the other side of that big ocean. For some strange reason, I remembered the coffin maker whom I hadn't seen in a very long time, giving me a lecture on the pitfalls of superstition in our modern age. The atmosphere in the airport could not have been more modern. Planes took off and landed all around me. What better time than this, to embrace modernity, I thought. Sadly, I embraced it in the most despicable way, one that I would later come to deeply regret. I went into the washroom, unbuttoned my shirt, removed all the amulets from around my neck, and tossed them in the wastebasket. Only then did I proceed to board my airplane.

Montreal

When I woke up, I was so physically exhausted that I couldn't move. I had found a room in the basement of a nice house, after spending my first few nights in a rundown motel, where the constant clamor from the adjacent rooms had made me so nervous that I was unable to sleep. In my new quiet room, I stayed in bed and slept for two days. On the third day, my landlady came down to investigate. I heard her footsteps on the wooden stairs leading down to my basement room and was startled when she knocked on the door. I was not ready to be seen, but her knocking grew louder, and I had no choice but to open the door. Taken aback when she saw me, she asked if I was sick. I said that I was fine, but didn't know what to do next, and I asked for help.

Embarrassed for not having my pajama top on, I returned to bed and covered myself with the blanket. After instructing me to stay in bed, Louise, my landlady, left the room for a few minutes and returned with a small tray containing a cup of coffee and a piece of toast. I had never had anything served to me in bed before, and it felt awkward. But the coffee tasted wonderful. It felt like a magical potion giving me two separate identities: one in bed sipping coffee and contemplating new adventures, and the other looking on and wondering what the person in bed might do next. I didn't know it at the time, but this split would become part of my new life. Seeing how helpless I looked, Louise offered to take me to the employment office. She suggested that I shower and put on fresh clothes. I was happy to obey her commands. I needed someone to lead me.

After showering, I opened my suitcase and began organizing my clothes. Choosing a shirt proved to be difficult, as all of them were gifts from family members whom I wanted to honor. I settled on a red paisley one given to me by Aunt Miriam. When I went up to Louise's kitchen, she smiled and asked me to sit, then she went to another room. I was amazed at how sterile everything looked. There was no aroma of food, but I didn't rush to the assumption that Louise didn't cook. I had already discovered, from the short time I'd spent in the Montreal airport, that this was a country where people masked odors. All the men and women wore perfume, and the washrooms at the airport didn't smell like washrooms. Even when I stood at the urinal, the white crystal in the bowl emitted a vapour that not only masked the smell of urine, but also temporarily erased my own sense of smell.

Louise returned to the kitchen moments later smelling like the people at the airport. It was disconcerting at first to live in this new sanitized atmosphere. In Nazareth, I could, with closed eyes, distinguish my mother by the spices she used in her cooking, and my father by the scent of wood shavings or shellac.

Once we boarded the bus, Louise took special care to explain to me the bus route, but the new scenery distracted me. At the employment office, a man read a list of available positions. Most of them were for office work, but there was one opening for a cutter in a clothes manufacturing company. Having helped my friend Nikoula at his tailor shop in Nazareth, I felt that I was qualified for the position. The job proved to be simple. I was trained very quickly, and the only thing I had to remember was to move my left hand out of the way before pressing the button that released the heavy upper portion of the industrial cutter onto the blade below. The press was situated in the middle of the factory floor, giving the women in the plant easy access to the cut fabric.

At the end of my first day, I stopped at a restaurant and ordered a hamburger, the only item on the menu that I knew. Aware of the long distance to Louise's house, but wanting to explore my new city, I decided to walk to my new home. Although it was a working day, the streets were busy with shoppers, who came out of stores carrying boxes and bags, an atmosphere only seen around holidays in Nazareth. Trying to understand the culture of my new city, I walked back to my room every day after work. Looking different from everyone around me didn't seem to present a challenge. In Haifa, I needed to put time and effort into how I dressed in the hopes of blending in with the newcomers, to avoid potential conflict. For the first time, I felt that I was equal to everyone on the street, at least under the law.

Although it was exciting to be in Montreal, it was difficult for me to understand my new culture. In Nazareth, the largest Palestinian town in Israel, I had been among family, neighbors, and friends. Knowledge of my culture had been handed down to me. Here, it was up to me to figure things out. Gradually, I began to suspect that not all inherited information was useful. It often came with a certain bias and a narrow tolerance for other traditions. I not only continued to struggle on my own, but I also began to like it that way. I spent most of my time exploring Montreal and didn't go to my room until I was tired and ready to crawl into my bed. It was there, in the dark, away from the dazzling lights of my new city, that my family and friends would appear in my dreams and stayed in my consciousness until it was time for me to return to work.

Aside from the owner and the foreman, there were only a few men at the plant. The owner sat in his office with a large window, where he could see everyone on the floor. The foreman walked around and didn't seem to have anything to do except intimidate the women who sat in rows working on their sewing machines.

At the end of one particular workday, a young woman named Jacqueline from the fashion department asked if I wanted to walk with her to the Metro station. Perhaps unable to pronounce the name Said, she called me Sid. Happy to be in her company, I tolerated the name change, and we continued to walk together to the Metro at the end of each day.

After a few weeks, Jacqueline invited me to her house for dinner. I accepted without hesitation. I was so happy to be with her that it was not until she left the kitchen that I noticed my surroundings. Although the kitchen was small, her place felt like a home—not like my room, which was only for sleeping, as I ate all my meals out. Still, I wondered why she had left her own family. After dinner, we went for a walk on her tree-lined street but did not say much to one another. I hoped that she would ask me about my past and the family I had left behind. But she didn't. I feared that my history would no longer be relevant to anyone in my new country.

A week later, Jacqueline asked if I would like to accompany her to a friend's house for dinner. She said that her friend Aida lived with her parents who were of Arab origin. I accepted happily, thinking they would be like my own parents. I looked forward to having kibbeh and tabbouleh, only to discover that they were serving hamburgers. I suspected that Aida may not speak Arabic but assumed that her parents would. I soon discovered that they too were born in Montreal. Their parents had come to Canada in 1910 from Lebanon. When the visit was over, I went to my room and sat on the only chair next to the bed. After a pleasant evening with good company, my room felt dull. I had thought of my subterranean room as a nice place to be, but now it felt bland and devoid of any visual stimulation.

That night I tossed and turned. I kept thinking about Aida's family and how Canadian they had become. They were like any other Canadian that I had met. Their knowledge of the Middle East was limited to what they heard on the news, and their Arabic culture had completely washed away. The thought saddened me, because I knew that this could one day be my fate if I stayed in Canada. I could have a child who wouldn't speak Arabic. I thought of how fragile identity can be. People fight wars to preserve it, and yet all it took, in Aida's family's case, was fifty-eight years to erase it. It was a sobering thought. I spent a lot of time that night analyzing my national identity and wondering whether it was worth dying for, as so many people did.

As winter approached, I began to appreciate my small room again. Outside, it was unbearably cold. I had come to tolerate its bleakness, for it fulfilled a new and different need: it kept me warm. Aware that I was spending most evenings at home, Louise asked if I would like to go to church with her on Sunday. I hadn't attended a church service for many years, but I accepted. Then she asked me to have lunch with her, and we spent time talking about Jesus. Because I was from Nazareth, Louise spoke as if I knew him personally when I described the holy sites that I used to walk past on my way to school. With tears rolling down her cheeks, she walked across the table and held me tight for a moment, then apologized and moved back to her seat. I didn't know what she was apologizing for but suspected that she felt that she was using my connection to Nazareth to save her soul. When the visit ended, she told me that it would be all right for me to watch television in her living room or use the kitchen if I needed to cook.

The following Sunday, she came down to my room and asked if I wanted to go to church. Afterward, our conversation again turned to religion. She asked me if I had ever been to the Jordan River. I told her that the Sea of Galilee was where I had first learned how to float when I was a little boy. That was before the sea was depleted by the Israeli irrigation project, which diverted water to the South. I described to her how wonderful it was to swim there when the water was so wonderfully pure. I also told her how, with my father's help, I swam among the reeds from the sea to the mouth of the Jordan River, where he taught me how to whistle through a blade of grass, and to drink water with my cupped hands. Tears welled up in her eyes again and she asked if I had ever written my memories down. I was startled by the question. "I'm not a writer," I said. "But if I were, I would write a whole book describing the Jordan River and the sweet fragrance that infused the air with a scent that I don't have words for." Suddenly the expression on her face changed, it was as though she had just discovered some earthly pleasure which she had not been aware of before.

I was always happy when the weekend ended. The friendly welcome I received on Monday morning energized me and made me feel that I belonged with the mostly emigrant women at the factory. Living alone, I was never excited when the bell rang to signal the end of the workday. However, the women, eager to return to their families, ripped their aprons off and ran to the exit. One by one, they punched their time-cards into the clock on the wall with great precision and relief. I stayed near my press and listened to the clock punching the timecards rhythmically and unceasingly.

In time, I stopped rushing back to my room, even when it was cold. I strolled through unfamiliar streets, and spent hours exploring department stores, looking at televisions that were stacked on top of one another, all projecting the same image. Unlike the market in Nazareth, where you had to buy something the minute you entered a store, in Montreal you could spend hours in a store without buying anything. No one seemed to mind. I began to spend much of my time in these stores just to avoid my room. I knew that it was a mere distraction, as I was still alone, even when I was surrounded by hundreds of people. However, I continued to crave the energy of the crowd. It defied all reason. I had thought that being in a big city would increase my chances of meeting people, but it seemed as though the people around me preferred their anonymity. I became aware of a new reality. The official welcoming immigration policy was only a bill of rights. The responsibility of becoming a full member of society was my own.

My efforts to pronounce words correctly often failed. I was quickly identified as an immigrant. At the plant, distinctions between immigrants were often overlooked. All newcomers were perceived to be the same. In this setting, who would ever associate me with my family and the beautiful house of my childhood? At the plant, my few Canadian co-workers perceived me to be similar to the newly landed Italian women. We all behaved similarly in our new environment. We shared the same reluctance when having to reveal ourselves. We doubted our old customs and values. We were not fluent enough in French or English and could not articulate our past lives.

Trying to win the acceptance of others, I smiled even when there was nothing to smile about. I was eager to help acquaintances, and sometimes I ran to help strangers, as was the case when I rushed to the aid of an old woman who was struggling to carry a suitcase on the Metro steps. She mistook me for a thief. My cultural etiquette was also misunderstood. The practice of not staring at a woman's face when speaking to her, a polite gesture in the Middle East, was perceived here as shifty or evasive. Even as my English began to improve, I still did not understand idioms that the locals used. Many years later, I still ask myself how I ever figured out that what seemed to be a question, "Is the pope Catholic?" was actually a statement—an emphatic "yes."

Encouraged by my willingness to spend time with her on other weekends, Louise came down to my room one Sunday and asked if I wanted to spend the day with her. She said that she had a surprise for me. Without asking for details, I said yes. We walked to the Metro station and took the train in a direction that was unfamiliar to me. I sat next to her as the train moved with alarming speed with much longer intervals between stations. At one station, Louise stood up and I quickly followed her. Climbing up to the earth's surface, I realized that we were on the grounds of Montreal's International Expo, which had ended the year before, in 1967, but was still operating under the new name of "Man and his World." We began by visiting the smaller buildings. Louise saved the American Pavilion for the end of the day. Mesmerized by its round shape, I stood there trying to understand how the large structure stood on the ground without visible means of support. It was beautiful beyond description: by far the newest and the most modern building that I had ever seen.

I was almost twenty-two when "modernity" had become the new slogan in Nazareth, and in many other countries in the region. Although many people didn't even know exactly what the word meant, they thought they wanted it. The moment they realized what it really meant, they abandoned the idea in favor of tradition. I, on the other hand, embraced it. My family was liberal, but only to a point. The family structure and the way we conducted ourselves within society was still traditional. Being around Louise and Jacqueline, I marveled at their independent lifestyle.

I was lost in such thoughts when Louise said that she was tired and asked me if I was ready to return home. However, after we returned to her house, she asked if I would like to come in for tea. As she went to the kitchen, my eyes wandered around to the rest of the house. I noticed that Louise had many things in the house that she never used. Her piano, her small settee in the hallway, and even her dining room furniture, looked as though they had never been touched. Here was another difference from Nazareth. There, people had only what they needed.

When Louise returned with the tea, I told her how much I had enjoyed my day. She said that she had too, but apologized for being a little quiet. She explained that she was suffering from severe headaches. It happened whenever she had too much excitement in her day. Smiling, she added, "You come from a place where healing by touch is possible. Do you think that you could help?" I was dumbfounded, as I didn't understand what she meant. She asked if I would massage her head. With a pounding heart, I walked over to where she was seated and placed my hand on her forehead. Thankfully, she closed her eyes. I was very nervous. Louise's skin felt very soft, and her blond hair was silky and smooth. As I massaged her head, she relaxed her face. I suddenly saw a much younger woman.

Louise was at ease, but, although I had her permission, I still felt uneasy about touching her.

When my visit was over, I walked down to my room and went straight to bed. Lying there, I tried to retrace the images painted on the ceiling of my childhood home in Nazareth. My mind wandered back to a dream I once had of finding gold behind the framed picture that hung in our living room. It was a picture of the bejeweled Mary, the painting that my father had loved the most in our house, even more than the angels painted on the ceiling. He loved it only for its artistic qualities, but my mother received its full benefits. She lit candles for it and believed that it answered her prayers. In my dream, I removed the painting that hung on a nail from the wall and discovered a small opening behind it containing real jewels like those in the painting. I remembered how excited I was when I told my mother about my dream. She decided it was an omen that needed to be investigated. There were rumors that some people in Nazareth had found treasures hidden in attics and walls, left by the frightened people who had to flee in haste during the war. On my mother's insistence, my father agreed to explore the wall behind the painting. As he worked at it with a hammer and a chisel, plaster dust flew everywhere. My mother didn't mind, treating the dust as if it were manna from heaven. The blows eventually revealed only a plain brick wall. I remembered the disappointment we all felt. I could almost hear my mother's voice still cursing the poverty and wars that turned reasonable people into fools.

My life in Montreal became solitary after Jacqueline suddenly left work and Louise reverted to being formal when

I stopped going to mass, despite her repeated invitations. Jacqueline and I stayed in touch, and every now and then went to see movies together. In time, my work became tedious and I began to contemplate a return home. The idea made me happy, but there was always a voice that told me not to return. This voice promised me that a new happiness was just around the corner. I held on to that promise, but felt increasingly restless as time went by. I began to think about moving to Toronto.

I waited until spring before quitting my job, then told Louise that I was moving. She said that she wished that I would stay and told me that she had been praying for me. But I never asked for her prayers, nor did I feel accountable to God. Unlike her, I didn't need a religious or scientific explanation for how and why I had arrived on this Earth. Like many young people in their early twenties, I had found answers to life's complex questions. I had everything figured out. I didn't believe in God or the afterlife, for which Louise had forfeited all her earthly pleasures. I was sure that death, when it came, would take me back to the same place from which I had come, a place where consciousness does not exist. A few days before my departure, I met with Jacqueline for dinner and informed her about my move. When it was time for us to leave the restaurant, she wrote her address on a piece of paper and made me promise to call her when I had settled down. Two days later, I packed my suitcase and left.

In contrast to Montreal, where everything appeared to be established, Toronto was quickly changing. Many large building projects were underway, which would potentially lead to good paying jobs. My new city, however, made me feel twice as removed from my family. Even though Toronto and Montreal were both relatively the same distance from Nazareth, being in Toronto felt different. There was a new and different memory between myself and Nazareth. The memory of Montreal had been added. As mundane as those memories were, they still had an effect on me. My intense longing for my family and friends in Nazareth was diluted, for other memories were now superimposed on it.

In my first few weeks in Toronto, Louise most often came into my memory. It bothered me to think that my mind chose to recall her more than my mother, but I rationalized that it was just a matter of proximity. Louise was miles closer to me than my mother. It was not that my devotion to my family had diminished, but rather that my memory had chosen to travel the shortest distance. At least, that is what I told myself. In reality, however, I feared that I was slowly being removed from what I considered to be my real life in Nazareth.

It took a while before I wrote to Jacqueline. I was very self-conscious about writing in English, but with the aid of a dictionary, I managed to write a short letter which included my address and phone number. The meanings of English words were never fully clear to me, as they were in Arabic. Familiar sensations were now replaced with new and foreign ones. Still, I consoled myself with the fact that I was living in peace.

This strange and magical inner tranquility was shattered in September of 1972 by the massacre of the Israeli athletes at the Munich Olympics. Suddenly, I was viewed as being somewhat responsible for something I hadn't done. I had been working at the University of Toronto for a company that was in charge of repairing and painting various buildings on campus. My Canadian co-workers unexpectedly began to talk to me about politics, and I felt a sudden change in their attitude toward me. They wanted me to tell them why those men had committed such an act. Lacking knowledge of the men's motivations, I was still expected to explain to them.

There had been so much distraction in my daily life that I had stopped thinking about my national identity. Now, it had become a liability, and I had to face unjustified hostility. Fortunately, this occurred the same week that I made a new friend. One morning, when I walked into the workshop at the physics building, a young blond man about the same age as me was waiting for my arrival. Together, we were assigned to paint the walls in a large lab filled with equipment and delicate glass flasks. Painting the lab was tedious, but we found ample time to converse. We soon discovered that our pasts had many parallels. His parents had fled their home in Estonia when his father lost his business during the Soviet invasion of their country, and they were deprived of their livelihood, as had my own family when my father's carpentry shop in Haifa was bombed during the clashes between Arabs and Jews. It did not take long for me to realize that, despite the color of our skin, we had many similarities. My friend did not have a memory of the Russian invasion of his country; he was not even born during those events. His mother had given birth to him in Sweden at a displaced persons camp. However, like me, he felt changed by his parents' tragedy. I came to understand that while painful firsthand experiences could be dealt with in time, inherited collective pain was much more difficult to reconcile.

My employer was seething when I met him at the end of the day. He wanted an explanation for the Munich massacre. When I didn't give him one, he paused and asked me the dreaded question: my own feeling about it. I could have told him that my guess was that when liberty is taken away from men and women, they become prone to acting in dangerous and destructive ways. But common sense prevailed, and I choose not to answer him. After that, I avoided contact with people. I stayed in my apartment after work and watched the news, but there was nothing in the news about the suffering of Palestinians. In fact, the media often reported Israeli attacks on Palestinians as if they were nothing more than minor infractions.

My co-workers quickly became experts on Islam. They wanted to know if I believed that virgins were waiting in heaven for those who commit acts of martyrdom. I didn't bother to tell them that I was not Muslim. Nor did I tell them that the Muslim friends and neighbors that I grew up with and loved did not believe or endorse such a concept. Everyone at work seemed to feel entitled to my innermost thoughts and beliefs. However, I soon discovered that most of them were upset because the murder had taken place at a sports event, which they regarded as sacred. Luckily for me, their anger only lasted until the next big hockey game, and they returned to their usual and happy lives. Even my employer felt regretful about his harsh interrogation, but I was left with the same apprehensions that I had lived with for most of my life.

Jacqueline and I stayed in touch for over a year. In time, our phone calls became less frequent, and eventually were reduced to special occasions and birthdays. Much of my time after work was spent at home reading or painting, something that I loved doing when I was a boy. I stopped eating out or going to the movies. This allowed me to save money, and I began to consider returning home more seriously. It would not be a permanent return, but just a visit with family and friends.

In 1976, at the age of thirty-one, I received a telegram from my mother asking me to return home. She said that my father was in critical condition. He had fallen from a scaffold at work. It took me one day to get everything ready, and with my employer's understanding, I left Toronto.

Upon my arrival in Tel Aviv, I was met with the usual harsh treatment that a Palestinian receives when returning home. I followed an official into a room for questioning. My interrogator was a young man about the same age as me. He brandished his authority without conviction. Still, I knew that I was unable to ask for sympathy or for a quick discharge. When I was finally released, I hired a taxi and asked to be driven to Rambam Hospital in Haifa. I could hardly believe that I would soon see my mother and the rest of my family.

Everyone was waiting outside by the main entrance. I hugged my mother who looked frail and vulnerable. I had to maintain my composure in the presence of my cousins and my uncles. I didn't bother to ask about my father, for the scene told me everything I needed to know. With nearly every paternal relative present, I understood the gravity of the situation. As we stood in silence, my cousin, who worked at the hospital, came out to greet me. He was the first family member to have graduated from medical school, to the immense pride of the entire family. After our embrace, he took me inside and introduced me to the surgeon, who explained in Hebrew that he had tried his best to save my father, but that his injuries were very serious, and that his chances of recovery were slim. He expressed extreme regret, directed me to where my father was, and left.

I walked in and saw my father's motionless body lying on a bed surrounded by a tangle of wires. A man with similar head injuries occupied the bed next to him. I exchanged sympathetic glances with the woman standing by his bed. My father didn't look like the father I had known. His face was badly injured and his chest, with the help of a respirator, rose and fell involuntarily. It bothered me that I didn't feel what I had expected to feel, and I reacted in anger. Did he not want to see me, or hear the stories that I had been carefully gathering for him while I was away? Still confused, I put my head between my hands and wept. Then, not wanting the woman who was standing next to her injured husband to see me cry, I left the room and went back downstairs and stood with my mother and the rest of my relatives. I wanted to kiss everyone and ask questions about their lives, but I knew that this wasn't the right time to do it. I felt as though I was being pulled in several different directions. I was angry and sad, but also much happier than I had been for the past few years. This made me anxious, and I wondered how I could be so happy when my father was on his deathbed. But, how could I not be, when everyone I had been missing for so long now surrounded me?

The vigil in the hospital lasted for ten days. Everyone went to their homes at night and returned in the morning, forming a line by the security gates before they could enter. Inside the hospital, Palestinians and Jews were generally pleasant to one another. I saw people behave in a civilized way I hadn't imagined possible. As I walked through the corridors, I could see Jewish and Palestinian doctors working side by side, providing help to people regardless of their ethnicity. It was as if the rules of conduct on the outside did not apply in here.

One day, I saw my mother sitting on a small bench, holding hands with the Ashkenazi woman, whose husband lay motionless beside my father.

That same week, both men died. The man next to my father died first. A few days later, in August 1976, my father had disappeared from his room when we returned in the morning.

I was given the task of identifying his body in the morgue. Everyone in the neighborhood came to the funeral, bringing chairs for one another. We placed my father in the middle of the room. As the oldest son, I sat next to his body and received people's condolences.

The fact that my father had died without seeing me by his side in the hospital made the women in the room weep frantically. They were repeating what I thought was a chant, but in fact it was more like a plea urging my father to wake up, because his oldest son was back from Canada. Soon their sobs became frenzied. Everyone looked at me in anticipation. They expected me to participate or talk to him as they did, but I remained silent, meeting the disapproving stares of everyone in the room. Embarrassed, I sat there feeling alienated from what was happening around me. I was no longer willing to participate in rituals. I wanted my grief for my father to be my own.

After the funeral, everyone went home except for Aunt Miriam and Uncle Subhe, my father's older brother. They stayed with us for two weeks. My aunt cooked and baked bread, while my uncle received people who came to offer their support and sympathy. We, the immediate family, spent each morning together with my aunt and uncle. In the morning, my mother would busy herself cleaning and sorting through my father's clothing, most of which was going to charity, except for the good suits that my mother offered to my uncle. He was in no mood to talk about clothing. She seemed anxious about my father's belongings and wanted them out of the house. It seemed to me that she was preparing for a fresh start. She may well have been dreading it, but she had never been one to postpone the inevitable.

When my aunt and uncle left, and things had settled down around the house, my mother began to make attempts at asserting herself. She took on small tasks, such as buying vegetables from the truck that came to our neighborhood. Before his death, my father went to the market and did the shopping. To honor her, he did all the chores that men considered inappropriate or too difficult for a woman to do. Ironically, women like my mother had accepted the honor and allowed their husbands to do many things on their behalf. In time though, I began to notice that she was becoming uncomfortable with her new responsibilities. She began to ask my youngest brother Aouni to shop for her.

Since I left home at a young age, I did not know my brother as well as I ought to, nor did I know my brother Souheil or my sisters Najla and Layla, who were married and had children of their own. Aouni was the last one at home, and I made a concerted effort to get to know him better. I had always loved my family and played with my brothers and my sisters when we were young. But quite naturally, our interest in each other diminished when we developed relationships with kids our own age. There was something exciting about being able to share feelings and talk about desires that one could not share with one's siblings. Then came a time in my teenage years when I wanted to break away from my family. I spent my evenings with my friends and didn't return home until midnight, unaware that I would be spending the rest of my life longing to return home.

Sitting with my mother and my younger brother was a great comfort to me after having lived alone for such a long time. Daily life felt pleasantly habitual. It did not need to be analyzed. Everything felt recognizable at a first glance. One day, I went with my brother Souheil to the market and saw him interact with others. Everyone knew who he was and could retrace his lineage. Grocers shared their memory of our father and sent greetings to our uncles. Even the walls in our town stood unchanged and still bore the stains left by the people that came before us. My brother didn't have to question his identity as I did when in Canada. He knew at all times where he was by looking at his eternal surroundings. My own environment in Toronto had no gravitational pull. I moved around the city with indifference and without a specific objective. Roads did not lead to a relative's house, or to the town square, where my friends would be waiting for me.

It was not long, however, that I realized that, although I was happy to be at home with my family, I still felt conflicted. I began to see that my life was now lived through the many customs and rituals required by our society's expectations. Mourning my father's death meant that we had to omit all the simple pleasures in our lives. To eliminate music, the radio had to be unplugged, and our conversation had to appear somber. My mother and two sisters wore black dresses, our reaction to people and events had to appear joyless, and our emotions had to be controlled. I loved my father and grieved his death deeply but having lived away from him and without these rituals, I felt restrained and longed for my return to Toronto. I hoped that the vast distance that separated these two cities would blur the imperfections and blemishes of my home that I began to notice and reject. It was a troubling feeling when I realized that I was no longer bound by the restrictions practiced in my society. I felt estranged from my own culture. I had become an impostor in my own country, and my feeling of isolation became similar to what I felt in Toronto.

One day, my mother asked about the date of my departure. I told her that I was waiting for the appropriate time before I made a decision. She looked at me and said that it was okay for me to leave whenever I was ready. I knew that she had been preparing for that eventuality, and it seemed as though she wanted to meet her grief all at once.

That same day, I drove to Shefa-'Amr to say goodbye to Aunt Miriam. She had moved out of the main house after her children had all married. She now lived in a separate small house that was built at the edge of her property, closer to the street, with a good-sized door, which she left open so she could greet friends and neighbors as they walked by. Above the couch, I noticed the postcard that I had sent to her when I first arrived in Montreal. It was still tucked into the lower part of a frame holding a picture of the Virgin Mary, with baby

Jesus on her lap. She was eager to talk to me, as we had not yet had a personal conversation. We hadn't wanted to offend my mother, who was in deep mourning, by having a casual chat.

She was eager to learn about my life in Canada, and asked me how it felt to be living among the *Franj*, a term used to indicate the crusading Franks. She also wanted to know if the *Franj* knew how to farm. I told her that I lived in a big city and didn't know. She said that farming was no longer a viable option for many Palestinian farmers in Galilee and lamented the loss of those skills.

A few days later, I packed my suitcase and spent the day at home in anxious anticipation. The following morning, a taxi came to pick me up. I hugged my mother and the rest of my family, then left without the fanfare of my original departure. I felt anxious as we approached the airport, worrying about the unpleasant treatment I was about to receive. Having lived in a country where authority could be challenged, I found it difficult to be submissive when dealing with Israeli officials. I handed my Israeli passport to the young security official, but my name identified me as a Palestinian. He looked at me as if puzzled by my appearance and by the fact that I spoke to him in English. I could tell that he was not comfortable with this image of an Arab. He had a preconceived notion in his head about us. Most Israelis know very little about the indigenous people living among them.

He asked me to follow him to a small room, where he began to ask all the required questions, which led to the opening of my suitcase. His puzzlement increased when he found an art book by Marc Chagall in my case. It was a book that I had bought in Haifa. I was surprised when he suddenly switched to English and asked me if I liked Chagall. "Yes, very much," I said. He paused a little and then asked if I knew that Chagall was Jewish. I told him that I was aware of that, but I liked his work anyway. He smiled, stopped his search, and explained to me that Marc Chagall was his favorite artist. Suddenly, our conversation felt like a talk between two friends. All my fears of hostility melted away. I found myself telling him that I was not a trained artist but that I loved painting, and that the few people I knew in Toronto felt that my work had the spirit of Chagall in it. Fascinated, he said, "Perhaps we'll meet again someday." He closed my suitcase, and I walked to my aircraft.

After returning from Nazareth, I was physically and emotionally exhausted, and had trouble adjusting to being alone. I kept thinking about my mother. The guilt I felt from leaving her would not go away. Unlike my first arrival in Montreal, which promised excitement and discovery, my return to Toronto made me aware of an undeniable truth. I became keenly aware of my own limitations and of the struggle that lay before me, which until then I had chosen to ignore.

When the phone rang in my apartment, I was startled, and imagined that it was a call from the rectory in Nazareth, since few people over there had a telephone, and most went to the church if they needed to use one. The call was from Jacqueline. My heart leapt in excitement even though I wanted to hold on to my sadness. Addressing me as *Sid*, she told me that she had been thinking about me and invited me to visit her. Her candor reminded me of the pleasant times we had together, and made her long absence seem brief. I wanted to tell her about my father's death but feared that the news would darken our reunion. I had not gone back to work yet and felt anxious about leaving Toronto again, but I hesitantly agreed to visit her on the weekend.

I was surprised by a feeling of exhilaration when the train left the station. Halfway to Montreal, however, my excitement turned to apprehension. Except for the platonic love I'd shared with a girl in Nazareth, and the brief relationship I've had with a girl in Toronto, I had limited experience with romantic love, and feared this was what Jacqueline had in mind. When I stepped down from the train, she was there waiting for me. As we walked together, I realized that her interest in me had grown in my absence. During the drive to her home, Jacqueline reminisced about our time together in the factory. I remembered how infatuated I was with her when we first met. But she seemed unattainable in those days. I reached over to touch her hair just to see how it felt. After dropping my small suitcase in her house, we spent the day revisiting places that we used to enjoy and didn't return until after we had dinner at a restaurant. We were in the car when I decided to tell her about my father's death and explained to her my initial reluctance when she called to invite me to visit her. Without saying anything, she stretched her arm in my direction and held my hand for a long time. It was nearly midnight when we returned to her home. The air inside felt cold, and Jacqueline quickly lit the wood in the fireplace and left the room. Trying to stay warm, I kept my jacket on and sat near the fire.

A fresh scent announced her return to the room, dressed in a beautiful nightgown. She looked like one of the Pre-Raphaelite women in a copy of a painting that my father had brought home one day and hung in the kitchen, despite my mother's objections. My pulse quickened. Then I remembered what my mother used to say to me on days when I was scheduled to visit a friend's house after school: "Even if you are famished, behave as if you have a full stomach when food is offered and accept your food with grace." Not wanting to appear too eager, I looked away. As she sat on the opposite side of the fireplace, I noticed how the glow of the fire lent her skin a rosy tone and made her look more beautiful than ever before. I looked at her long and slender legs and felt that all the signs were clear that I was hers and she was mine for the night. I felt nervous at first, but I soon discovered how effortless it was for me to love her.

I woke up the next morning only to find out that I was alone in bed. Realizing that it was late, I took a quick shower and put my clothes on and left the bedroom. I found Jacqueline playing her piano. I had only thought of her as a young woman who was my equal, a worker like myself, but now I realized that she had skills I didn't have. I felt awed by her musical talent and wished that I could offer her more. After breakfast, we spent the day talking and getting to know each other. Soon it was time for me to leave and she drove me back to the train station. We stood on the platform clutching hands and wishing that we could spend more time together. She offered me words of encouragement and promised that she would visit me often and made me promise to do the same.

Because I'd been a hard worker, my employer took me back when I called him upon my return from Montreal. He was happy to hear from me and understood my need to be at my father's funeral.

A month after my visit to Montreal, Jacqueline called to say that she was coming to visit me. In her presence, my apartment felt unusually comfortable. We enjoyed cooking and eating together and even the simple act of washing dishes with her felt exciting. Except for the walks we took in my neighborhood, we spent the whole weekend in my apartment.

After Jacqueline left, I knelt on a cushion in front of the coffee table to write a letter to my mother. My letters to her were becoming less frequent lately. I hadn't mentioned Jacqueline yet, and was tempted to write something about her, but I was afraid of her reaction. I wondered if she would be happy to hear that I was in a relationship with a Canadian woman, or if she would think that my relationship with Jacqueline was my biggest betrayal to my country and my culture. I wrote about my work, and the ingredients that I used for my cooking. I refrained from writing about the abundance of food. I reflected on my first visit to the supermarket in Toronto, where I had seen hundreds of tins of sweetened condensed milk displayed on the shelves. I remembered the excitement that one tin of it had generated in my entire family when we received it from a UN agency after the war. I bought one tin for myself, only to discover that it wasn't as good as when it was savored by my entire family. I liked the abundance of food in my new country, but I also realized that it made all things less precious. After completing the letter, I sealed it, and looked for a stamp that didn't bear a picture of Queen Elizabeth. My mother usually went to the same trouble, avoiding stamps depicting Moshe Dayan, or Golda Meir, looking instead for one depicting a flower from the Galilee hills.

Jacqueline's calls became more frequent after her visit. She encouraged me to move back to Montreal, but the notion of moving again made me anxious. I liked my comfortable apartment, and my familiar job, but I promised to think about it. I reflected on the benefits of having her in my life. I would not have to miss her anymore. Though I wondered if it would be a good thing. Missing her and looking forward to seeing her had become part of my daily routine. In the end, my desire to be with her won out. I decided to take two weeks off and called to say that I was planning to visit her on the weekend.

Jacqueline and I spent the early morning shopping for snow boots for me, and food to take with us to her parents' home in the country where we had planned to spend our time together. But something came up, and Jacqueline had to postpone our drive and went to see her mother. After she left the house, I walked to the Jewish deli on Boulevard Saint-Laurent and ordered smoked salmon on a bagel, something I had loved when I worked in Haifa. The atmosphere in the deli was familiar and oddly comforting. Even the Hebrew spoken by some of the patrons sounded like music to my ears. How strange, I thought, to be reminded of home in that way.

Upon my return, Jacqueline was waiting for me, and we drove to her family's small country home. A pristine white blanket of snow stretched out and covered everything around us. The scene reminded me of the desert. One color alone seemed to dominate the others, and it was up to my eyes to decipher the subtle hues created by shadows that gave per-spective to the otherwise uniform surroundings. The small old clapboard house was white and blended with the snow around it. A large shed close to the river leaned toward the water as if it had grown tired of its location and wanted to float somewhere else. We spent the first few days cooking and going on long walks. I reveled in this new and unaccustomed kind of freedom.

One week into our stay, the phone rang. Jacqueline answered and sat quietly with the receiver pressed close to her ear, nodding her head. She did not speak until it was time for her to hang up. I heard her say, "I will come right away." She then moved close to me and without emotion explained to me that her father had died. She sat at the piano and began to play with tremendous vigor. Although I had behaved in an unemotional way when my father died, I still found it difficult to watch her play music. In my mind, music was for pleasure. I initially feared that I was with an unfeeling person, only to discover the complexity of grief. When she stopped playing, a transformation took place. In a calm and gentle way, she explained that she wanted to be with her mother so they could attend the funeral of her estranged father.

Without Jacqueline, the house felt remote. My watch stopped and I didn't bother to rewind it. Everything around me stood still. The fire died, taking with it the only sound that had provided some relief. In the evening, I stayed in the chair, as the idea of going to bed on my own felt lonely. Soon, I fell asleep.

The brightness of the morning sun flushed out the darkness. It was visible even through my closed eyelids. I went into the kitchen, made a pot of coffee, and sat by the window looking at my white surroundings. I moved through the house, noticing things I hadn't seen on the previous days. I looked inside closets and encountered the musty smell of old photographs left on shelves behind closed doors. As if trying to escape their imprisonment, the photos had begun to self-destruct and fray around the edges. Looking closely, I realized that, without color, the black-and- white photos made her ancestors, and those that I'd seen of my own, look the same. Feeling like an intruder for having opened the closet, I carefully placed the pictures back on the shelves and went out for a walk.

The stillness of the undisturbed cold landscape made me feel uneasy at first, but then I was excited by seeing the deep tracks my footsteps had left. I ran ahead, happily making as many footprints as I could. This was the strongest reminder of my existence. It was not the first time that I had questioned my new reality in Canada. The confusion I felt about my identity deepened, for the answer was never clear. I was a Palestinian. I was an Arab, but my family was Melkite Catholic in a church where Greek was used for prayers on Sundays. I prayed in French at school on weekdays. Hebrew was the language I used outside my home in Nazareth, and now I was trying to embrace another language and a completely new and different culture. Having lived under Israeli martial law, and having suppressed a sense of national identity, I never had a clear understanding of how it might feel to be a Palestinian. Yet even now, after fifty-two years of living in Canada, I know without a doubt that the affinity that I feel for my Palestinian culture continues to be the most tangible source of comfort in my life.

After walking in the snow for what seemed like hours, I decided to turn back. Realizing that the imprints made by my footsteps were beginning to disappear under the falling snow, I was struck with panic. I ran back toward the old house, trying to retrace my footprints before they completely disappeared.

I was relieved when the house reappeared in the distance. Exhausted, I went back to the rocking chair and waited for the phone to ring. Jacqueline had been gone only two days, but I felt nervous and lost without her. I was not familiar with life in the country. I felt stranded. I couldn't wait to return to Toronto and to my more familiar surroundings.

I was still sitting in the rocking chair when Jacqueline's car appeared in the driveway. I was happy and relieved to see her, but I had already made my decision to stay in Toronto. For the next few days, Jacqueline and I tried to make the most out of our time together, but I could sense her anguish about being away from her mother. I didn't know how to offer her solace and suggested that perhaps we should return to Montreal. She was relieved and thanked me for my understanding.

I began to feel anxious about being away from work but decided to stay in Montreal for one more day, and visited Louise, my previous landlady. She seemed pleased when I called and invited me for lunch. In her house, she asked if I was happy in Toronto and inquired about my life. I told her that I had been away in Nazareth for my father's funeral. She began to cry. It appeared to me as though she was crying for someone she had personally known. I was touched, and reached for the rosary in my pocket. It was a rosary that I had bought in Nazareth, with her in mind. Moved, she held it close to her heart. Examining the beads, she wondered what they were made of. I explained that they were olive pits ground on both sides by Palestinian children. They rubbed them on rocks all day long as penance for sins they had never committed, then sold them to souvenir shops that used the pits to make rosaries. She still didn't understand, and I had to explain to her that by rubbing both ends off, the pit becomes a bead, enabling a string to go through it. She became visibly upset. Not wanting to be part of the children's pain, she placed the rosary on the table next to her. Suspecting that she was not going to use it, I told her that I had rubbed off the ends of pits myself when I was a boy and had survived. I stretched my hands out for her to see. "I'm sure the hands of my young cousins have touched some of those beads. Please use it and pray for them." Louise retrieved the rosary and placed it back close to her heart. I was happy to be with her, for she continued to live in my thoughts despite our religious differences.

Traveling back on the train to Toronto, I felt gloomy and couldn't understand my own feelings, especially when I began to miss Jacqueline. The next morning, I returned to my building repairs and painting work. Because I lived close to the Annex, I spent my evenings exploring Bloor Street, often eating out or listening to music at the Brunswick House, a popular tavern in the area. Other times, I would walk over to Yonge Street, past the Royal Ontario Museum, where a small group of indigenous men begged for change. They seemed to me as if their essence had been extracted. Their gaunt and disheveled appearances made them invisible to pedestrians, who sped by as if they were not there at all. I gave them my loose change whenever I could, and it was not long after that, they began to engage me in conversation whenever I walked by, and always wished me the best of luck when we parted. In time, I began to enjoy my encounters with them. They were the only people who acknowledged me in a city where I was a stranger. I stopped taking the subway home from St. George station, choosing instead to walk by the museum just for the joy of seeing them and for being recognized on the street. Wanting to know more about their history, I asked them a few personal questions, but they only offered back pleasantries. After several encounters, I began to see myself in them. I remembered being in Haifa, the city of my birth, and feeling bewildered and alienated from the foreign culture that had imposed itself on me.

My thoughts were always on my mother. I wondered how she was managing without my father. I knew that my youngest brother Aouni was with her, but being her oldest son, I often felt that I had shrugged off my responsibility. Home was never far from my mind, as it was always on the Canadian news. Watching from this side, it always looked as if the Palestinians were the aggressors and not the victims. Israel had many advocates in the West, actively remaking its image, while most Palestinians were still living in the hope that the rest of the world would someday learn the truth about their plight and come to their aid. Watching from afar was maddening. While I did escape physical hardships by coming to Canada, I could not escape the mental torment of having to witness the conflict from afar. I was haunted by my separation from my family and friends and began to question my reasons for leaving Nazareth. These feelings made my relationship with Jacqueline difficult. I stopped calling her as often, even when I missed her. Although we continued to talk on the phone for a while, Jacqueline eventually realized that I had no desire to move back to Montreal, and our relationship ended.

My Mother's Visit

I was thirty-five, when I received a letter from my brother Souheil informing me that our mother had been diagnosed with ovarian cancer. Her prognosis for survival was not promising, and he asked me to return home. Overwhelmed, I sat in my apartment and wept. Although my mother was still alive, I felt orphaned by her imminent death. Arriving in Nazareth, I walked under the cover of darkness, retracing my habitual path to my grandmother's house, where I was told my mother would be. Upset about being disturbed, dogs that had greeted me on my last visit now snarled and flashed their teeth in anger. Everyone in the family was up and waiting for my arrival. My uncle Jamil and his family had continued to live in the house after my grandparents' death, but everyone still referred to the house as our "grandparents' home." I was happy to be in a home that had provided me with so many happy memories, but now the house was guarding a secret in one of its rooms. My mother's illness was never mentioned by its Arabic name *saratan*. It was referred to as the unmentionable disease, instead of its proper Arabic name. I surmised from my conversation with my relatives that my mother's illness was not to be disclosed to non-family members. Cancer was considered by many in Nazareth to be a genetic flaw that could have serious and negative implications for families with sons and daughters eligible for marriage.

Distressed by these old superstitious beliefs, I hid my anger and asked to see my mother. To my surprise, she was sitting up in her bed waiting for me. Although four years had passed since the death of my father, she was still in a black dress mourning his death. She looked thin and frail.

Although she had always been a physically delicate woman, her appearance reflected not only her ailing body but also her broken spirit. I could also sense that the disease made her ashamed and that she wanted to apologize for it. I embraced her, then sat at the foot of the bed and asked about her condition. Her answer came in the form of quiet tears at first. Then she said that she had *saratan,* using the full Arabic name for cancer. The mere mention of it brought a look of defiance to her face. She said that everyone was hiding the news of her illness, not only from neighbors and friends, but also from her. Family members did not disclose the truth about her diagnosis. Still, she acknowledged their kindness for trying to shield her from despair.

My mother was not fluent in Hebrew. Communication with her doctors in Haifa was conveyed to her through my brothers and other relatives, who chose to tell her that she had a curable stomach condition. Being the oldest male child in our culture meant that I had been second in command to my father. Because he was dead, I had to assume his rank ahead of my two older sisters. With my father gone, my mother looked to me for advice. That same night, I made a decision to move her back to her home. We packed her suitcase, and my uncle drove us home.

In her own house, she immediately resumed her nurturing roll. She was no longer the frail bed-ridden woman. In the morning, she made breakfast, and I looked on in amazement at her sudden transformation. In control of her own home, and happy to have me with her, she began to respond positively to her radiation treatment. Two months into my visit, her cancer appeared to be in remission, and life returned to normal.

I resumed contact with old friends. I sat in coffeehouses and visited relatives. I was doing the things that I had been missing while in Canada. Family members spoke of the miraculous and healing power of my visit, and I began to feel the weight of my new responsibility. I became immersed in my new duties, which included shopping at the market for food. I never haggled and always paid what the vendors asked. This made them slightly suspicious of me, as it indicated that I was not familiar with the local culture and was viewed as a stranger among them. I was even spoken to in English on one occasion, which I found puzzling. Except for my long hair and jeans, I still looked the same as everyone else. I realized that a change had taken place in the way I behaved. My manners were different. With this new awareness, I was increasingly uncomfortable, even more than I had been on my last visit. The greatest acknowledgment of this transformation came when I was returning on the bus from Tel Aviv one day. At a roadblock that was set up by the Israeli military, they stopped the bus. They identified the Palestinian passengers and asked them to step down for questioning. Yet, I was left on the bus, disguised under my new and mysterious veil. My initial relief at having been spared the harassment turned into a most terrible feeling. For the rest of my visit, I felt detached from all aspects of my life.

My mother, on the other hand, became interested in the years I had spent away from home. Her questions were direct, and she listened intently to my accounts. Sensing her curiosity, I asked if she would like to visit Canada for a while, and, to my surprise, she said yes. She had never traveled beyond her normal radius of a hundred miles, and the prospect of traveling on an airplane to a faraway land excited her.

Our travel plans included a stop in Belgium to visit my oldest sister's son, who was at a university in Brussels. From there, we traveled to London and spent three days visiting the many obligatory sites on every tourist itinerary. In Toronto, my mother kept busy cooking and making the apartment comfortable. She learned to shop for food in the neighborhood. She reorganized my kitchen, bought new bed sheets and proper bath towels, and made curtains for the windows. Soon, my apartment took on a different look and feel. On our second weekend in Toronto, I took her to see the new city hall building, were she saw a mounted policeman in the square. The scene took her back to a time when the British police roamed the streets of Haifa harassing people and arresting suspected rebels. She was reminded of when she was young and newly wed, but also of the bitterness of having never lived in her own country as a free citizen. Although she was cautious around the policeman on the horse, she continued to look in his direction. As we stood there and watched, he dismounted his horse and as if on a mission, walked toward a small child who was running around in the city square, then knelt down to tie the child's shoelaces. I suspect that for most pedestrians present that day the scene was unremarkable. But it signaled an incredible and reassuring change for my mother.

Our outings to the countryside were her most enjoyable excursions. She loved to identify wild grasses and flowers, which she compared to plants that grew around Nazareth.

Unlike me, she managed to find a resemblance in most of her encounters with people. Often, I couldn't see them, but I began to feel them. I looked forward to going home at the end of my workday. My apartment began to smell like our home in Nazareth. Delicious aromas wafted from the kitchen, and joyful memories of earlier times in my childhood were summoned when the copper pots that my mother brought with her began to clank.

Having my mother as a witness, my life in Toronto felt legitimate. Everyday activities became meaningful. The simple act of shopping for food felt purposeful, and I was able to see my surroundings with unaccustomed clarity. Unlike people who mistook my lack of fluency in English for dim-wittedness, my mother saw me as the clever son who had managed to escape the hardships of everyday struggles that many Palestinians endure under Israeli rule. She was happy, and relished in her new experiences. Her life felt renewed. It seemed like the distance that separated her from home also reduced her worries about her cancer.

Our evening routine included walks in the neighborhood. I watched as her energy returned. She also began to regain her lost weight, but she still wore her black dress. I remember asking her one evening if she would consider giving up her black clothes and purchasing new and more cheerful clothing. After thinking about it for a while, she looked at me and said, "I loved your father very much, but maybe it is time for me to end this display of mourning." On my day off, I took her to a store and bought her new clothes. I was also able to convince her to cut and color her hair. Gradually, she learned to venture out beyond our immediate neighborhood. She enjoyed being in Toronto, loving the ease of being in a society that did not expect or demand conformity.

My mother stayed with me for nearly one year. One evening, during our routine walk, she said that it was time for her to return home. I had not anticipated her departure and did not know what to say. I asked her if she was lonely in Canada. She said that her visit would always be one of the happiest periods in her life, but that her home was calling her again. Although I was happy to have her with me, I didn't try to stop her. I knew that she was missing her familiar life and the many people that she had left behind. On our final day together, she took tremendous care when wrapping and matching gifts that suited her grandchildren's personalities and tastes. Aware of the possibility that we might never see each other again, we didn't speak. We pretended as if nothing could materialize without spoken words, and that we would remain in the present. To ensure her safe travel, I had chosen to fly her back on El-Al, the Israeli airline that flew directly from Toronto to Tel-Aviv. Since I couldn't escort her beyond the restricted area, I asked if someone from El-Al could assist in getting her on the airplane. A young woman wearing a uniform appeared moments later and guided her through the terminal. I walked by her side in the permissible zone until we reached the sliding doors. After a quick embrace, the doors parted, and my mother followed the young woman. I stood there, hoping to give my mother a final wave, but the doors quickly closed, and she disappeared.

Several months after her return, I received a letter from my sister Layla telling me that our mother was back in the hospital. We stayed in constant touch. I wrote long letters, which my sister answered skillfully, using adjectives that I knew were meant to soften a grim situation for my sake. On May 24, 1980, I walked into my apartment and saw the red light flashing on my answering machine. It was my brother Souheil calling from the rectory in Nazareth to announce the death of our mother. Since my family and relatives were still without phones at that time, I could not call back. All I could do for the first few days was write letters and cry. With the death of my mother, our family's home was forever gone.

Forty years after my mother's visit, at the age of seventy-five, much has changed for me in Canada. Life here with my wife, daughter, and son has brought me great joy. And yet, the unsettling awareness of being homeless has never fully gone away. I feel an ever-present sense of loss over what has happened to our family and community, and to Palestine.

ACKNOWLEDGMENTS

Writing this book has brought me together with wonderful and talented people.

To my wife Nella Fiorino, and my daughter Isabel and son Jamil, I am ever grateful for your loving encouragement, discerning taste, and support. To my nieces Ghada and Nouha, my warmest thanks for helping me verify historical facts.

My sincere thanks to Isabel Huggan for helping me develop my manuscript and for supporting me throughout the entire process; to my friend Dr. Bjarnason for invaluable computer assistance; to the late Patricia Bishop, who edited the earliest draft and got me started on the right track; and to Jonathan Ullyot, for ensuring that it was ready to be seen by a publisher.

At Interlink Publishing, my appreciation to Michel Moushabeck, my publisher for taking me on and for making himself available whenever I needed his help; to John Sobhieh Fiscella, whose editorial skills and judgment put me at ease and helped make this project truly enjoyable; and to Pam Fontes-May for her design sensitivity.

Lastly, thank you always to my mother Marie, who taught me the art of storytelling, and to my father Jamil, who instilled in me the love of reading.